WHITE AS SNOW

To Cheryl &
Jeremy ~
I hope you enjoy the
story. Have a Merry
Christmas.

Because He Lives!
Donna Gallup
12/4/06

WHITE AS SNOW

⋙ A Christmas Story ⋘

Donna Westover Gallup

CLADACH
Publishing

To
Daddy, who taught me to love the old west ~
Mama, who taught me to love the Lord ~
and my husband, who brought me to Colorado, where I love both.

WHITE AS SNOW : A CHRISTMAS STORY
Copyright © 2006 by Donna Westover Gallup
All rights reserved.
Published by CLADACH Publishing
P.O. Box 336144 Greeley, CO 80633
www.CLADACH.com
Printed in the United States of America

Cover Art: "Winter Cover-Up" painting by Dan Young
www.danyoungstudio.com

Library of Congress Control Number: 2006927465
ISBN-13: 978-0-975961-94-0
ISBN-10: 0-975961-942

Though your sins be as scarlet, they shall be as white as snow.

Is. 1:18

1864
Colorado Territory

1

THE SOUND OF THE WIND SENT CHILLS up Charlie's spine. He crouched inside his grandpa's barn, trying to ignore the haunting sounds that never used to bother him. He'd been living with his grandparents on this ranch since he was three years old. It's true that some things had been different since Grandma died, but as long as his big, strong Gramps was with him, Charlie wasn't ever afraid. Everything was different now, though. The old man hadn't woke up for two weeks. He just lay there in his bed with his eyes closed and his mouth open. Now Charlie shivered as the wind wailed round the corners of the barn.

The small ranch, with its cabin, barn, corral and out-buildings was nestled at the base of a hill and shadowed by a great mountain range that separated the entire Colorado territory northward. Charlie felt as if his home stood on the boundary between two different worlds. Eastward stretched the open prairie. Like a sea of rolling grasses dotted with rafts of scrub oak and prairie brush, it tossed its unmanned crafts through fluid green waves, eventually cascading over invisible cliffs of the blue horizon. In contrast, westward rose tree-covered hills, rolling and climbing upon themselves, silently erupting into the majestic Rocky Mountains, whose solid, snow-covered pinnacles ever pointed skyward.

As if determined to join the two contrasting scenes, the wind often swept across the prairie and whistled through the trees. A fellow could imagine the sonata of a lone wolf rolling up through the hills. Or he'd hear a mysterious siren song call across the grassy waves and intertwine itself in the limbs of the dark evergreens and golden aspens, then build to an eerie crescendo, only to fall to a sigh of rustling leaves and then recede, pulled back by an invisible tide. Catching the wind in their branches, the trees would sway and moan, as if mocking the wind's futile attempts to join prairie and mountains.

It wasn't just the crazy sounds that scared Charlie. There was something else in the wind. These days the gusts carried a threatening chill. Winter was coming, getting closer every day now.

Charlie stood up straight, heaved a big sigh and wiped the sweat from his forehead. He picked up one end of a heavy wooden beam. He'd have to start being the man around here and figure out how to do all the things that Gramps always did to prepare for winter.

"This is the last one," he muttered. He lugged the beam out the barn door, past the well, to the corral just as he'd done with the other six beams, leaving another furrow in the dirt behind him. Chickens fluttered and squawked in protest of the interruption to their endless pecking. Undaunted, Charlie continued his mission. At the fence, he jerked the end of the rail up with both hands and wiggled it back and forth until it finally slid into the notch of the fence post. Then he did the same thing at the other end.

"Done," he said and wiped his forehead again, looking at the fence with some measure of satisfaction.

Off in the distance, thunder rumbled as clouds thickened. Then lightning flashed and within seconds, thunder drummed across the prairie again, rolling up through the hills, then fading into the coldness of the dark clouds overhead. With the thunder following so close on the heels of the lightening that time, Charlie knew the storm had nearly reached his door. He scrambled to pick up the tools and run them to the barn. Then, just as he reached the cabin door, the sky opened and released the rain that had been building all day.

Rain pounded the little window of the cabin. Rivulets of water ran down the glass pane. Wincing at the pain in his hands, Charlie struck a match on the side of the fireplace and lit an oil lamp to get a better look at his blisters. His grandpa's work gloves were so big that he had opted not to wear them while he repaired the fence. But now he had to pay the consequences. Blood blisters nestled between his fingers and bubbled onto his palms, and wood splinters had embedded themselves deep into his skin. He went to the cupboard and, using fingertips and elbows, managed to pull down a tin box.

Charlie rummaged through the buttons, pins, and thread spindles until he found a large sewing needle. Grasping the eye he rested the sharp end on a hot cinder at the edge of the fireplace. Within seconds the tip glowed bright orange and he knew it was clean. He sat at the table and, taking a deep breath, began to dig into the skin of his palm with the sharp, blackened needle. Sometimes he had to open blisters to retrieve the tiny daggers, causing him to yelp out loud. Then he'd allow his mind to wander back over the day.

"Guess I shoulda tried to cut more firewood instead," he said, "but if I didn't fix that fence the cows coulda found their way out and prob'ly been ate by a grizzly or somethin'. Then Gramps woulda been disappointed in me for lettin' our money supply go to waste."

Each fall, Gramps sold a bunch of cattle, then soon after that he'd hitch Bessie to the wagon and he and Charlie'd take the day's ride to Pueblo and buy what they needed for the year in the way of farm tools, food supplies, dry goods, boots and jeans. Any extra cash went into a tin canister to be saved for "a rainy day." He and Gramps had sold forty head of cattle a few weeks ago, but they hadn't taken their trip to town yet, because Gramps got sick. Charlie sure hoped Gramps would wake up pretty soon. He didn't know what supplies they needed for winter, or how to hitch Bessie to the wagon, or even how to put a saddle on her.

2

CHARLIE FROWNED AND DUG DEEPER
with the needle. This splinter was a bugger. The hole in
his hand filled with blood until he could hardly see what he
was doing. He gritted his teeth and kept digging until the
needle finally brought out a tiny piece of wood. He stared
at the culprit. How could such a little thing cause so much
hurt?

The day the soldiers came to buy the cattle had been
the last really fun day Charlie could remember. The sergeant and his men were from the 9th Kansas Cavalry sta-
tioned at Fort Collins up north. Charlie was so excited to
see real soldiers in their uniforms and all on fine horses; he
followed them around and found out all he could.

The sergeant walked with a limp. Charlie overheard
the sergeant telling Gramps that he'd been injured in a
battle in Arkansas, and the army had transferred him to
the outpost of Camp Collins to protect travelers using the
Overland Trail as they headed farther west. Seems there'd

been some trouble between the Colorado Volunteer Regiment and the Cheyenne around Sand Creek. Before the sergeant could tell the story in details too graphic, though, Gramps had scooted Charlie back towards the cabin, out of earshot. But Charlie managed to lollygag and he heard every word about the bloody massacre.

Now Charlie stopped digging with the needle and sucked the blood out of the hole in his hand. He smiled to himself, remembering how he had sat on the cabin doorstep and watched the cattle negotiations. Gramps had folded his arms across his chest, dug in his heels, and refused to accept the army's low offers for his good beef. The soldiers soon learned that the old man wouldn't wear down easily. Growing frustrated, they slapped their hats against their legs and thrust their arms into the air like geese on a frozen pond. Although he was just beyond earshot, Charlie was pretty sure the soldiers were uttering words that would never be repeated in *this* house. But Gramps had remained calm. Eventually, they came to terms and settled on a fair price, sealing the deal with handshakes. The soldiers gave Gramps the cash on the spot and agreed to come back next fall.

After the price had been settled and paid, Gramps let Charlie perch himself on the top rail of the corral and watch the soldiers round up the small herd of Herefords. The white faces of the cattle bobbed up and down in a sea of brown prairie grass as puffs of steam bellowed from their nostrils into the cool, fall air. They moaned low and sorrowful-like.

The sergeant limped over and leaned against the rails of the corral next to Gramps and Charlie. "It's good to do business with you, Mr. Smith. And after travelin so far, me and the men appreciate the hospitality you've extended."

Gramps wiped his forehead with the back of his sleeve. "I appreciate the business, Sarge." Gramps tilted his hat back. "It's quite a trip down here for you and your men. Can't you find beef from a rancher somewhere up north, closer to your camp?"

The sergeant pursed his lips, giving thought to the question. "It's not too settled up around those parts yet. Lots of folks pass through, headin' out to Oregon mostly, but a few squatters stay in the area, and they usually do settle pretty close to the army posts—Fort Vasquez, Fort Morgan, Camp Collins—actually, we just moved the camp to a new location and changed the name to *Fort* Collins. Comin' up in the world." The sergeant winked at Charlie, then continued his explanation.

"There's some farmers growin' crops, but not much cattle yet. I 'magine it's only a matter of time, though, with all that open grassland available, and the buffalo startin' to dwindle."

Gramps wiped a bead of sweat from his temple. "How many men do you have at your camp, er fort?"

"Two hundred. And they've gotta eat," continued the sergeant. "Guess we could hunt buffalo, but we're not too keen on goin' out on the prairie, with the Indians all riled up."

"Can't say as I blame you," muttered Gramps.

The sergeant relaxed against the fence again and looked around. "Just you and the boy here, huh?"

"Yep, that's what it's come down to now, just me an' the young'n here." He reached his big hand up to Charlie on the fence and ruffled his hair, then he looked back at the sergeant. "We came out from St. Louie in '42, just me and my wife, Beth, and our boy, Teddy, who was this boy's pa.

The sergeant nodded and glanced around again at the neat, snug little ranch. He turned back to Gramps with respect in his eyes. "You've done wonders with this place, Mr. Smith. I'm sure it wasn't easy for a woman to live out here, though, raisin' a child and all."

"Naw, but Beth was tougher than she looked." Gramps stared at the prairie, lost in thought. "I tell ya what, she was a pretty little thing. Met her at a church social when she was just seventeen. I was twenty-one and not much to look at. But for some reason she looked twice and the rest is history."

The sergeant smiled and nodded.

Gramps continued, "She really didn't wanna leave all the family she had in St. Louie, but I'd had enough of the city. It was sprawlin' and encroachin' on our fam'ly farm, and I needed more breathin' room. She took care of the young'un and worked hard right alongside me for all those years and helped make this place what it is now."

"It's quite a legacy to leave your grandson someday. And I'd say he looks like a right handy little ranch boy."

"That's right, he sure is." Gramps grinned at Charlie, then turned back to the sergeant. "I thought my son'd take

14

to this life, too, but he didn't want any part of farmin'. Grow'd up and went back to St. Louie, went to school, got married, and settled down there."

"Well, the frontier life's not for everyone. My home is in Kansas City, and my wife and daughters like it there just fine, but they say that's far enough west for them. I'll feel better about them being there, though, when the confederates stop their bushwhacking along the border."

"I'm sure you will. I know a couple of men in Pueblo who headed back to their home states in the east to fight for the union. No one's heard any word from them for months. I sure been prayin' ev'ry day for Mr. Lincoln and U.S. of A. When the war's finally over, then maybe Congress can give more attention to makin' this territory into a state."

The sergeant nodded, looking serious as he stared at the fluffy clouds traveling across the blue sky. Maybe he was remembering the battles he'd taken part in before being sent to Fort Collins.

The soldiers had herded the cattle out into the open and were ready to hit the trail. Their shrill whistles split the air as the cattle bemoaned the trip ahead.

The sergeant gave his men an answering wave of his hat, then turned back to Gramps. "Just one more thing, Mr. Smith."

Gramps raised his bushy eyebrows in response.

"My commanding officer, Colonel John Humphries, asked me to offer you his greetings and condolences."

Gramps thought for a moment, then a wide grin spread

across his face slow and easy. "You don't mean Johnny Humphries?"

The sergeant cleared his throat and transferred his weight from one foot to the other. "Yes, sir, he's Colonel John Humphries now."

"Well, I'll be," Gramps exclaimed. "Sure, I know Johnny. I met his pa in Georgia back in 18 'n 12 when we served t'gether in the Creek War. Slim 'n me still get word to each other once in a long while, but I ain't seen his little towheaded Johnny in a month of Sundays. Colonel, huh? Not doin' too bad, then, I reckon."

The sergeant nodded and glanced over at his men, who looked anxious to get going, trying to keep the herd together while they waited. He stood a little stiffer and limped to the fence post and untied his horse's reins, preparing to mount. "Yes, Colonel Humphries is doing just fine, Mr. Smith. He's the one who suggested we come down here and inquire about your cattle. Seems his pa mentioned you had a small ranch and we should consider buyin' from you."

Gramps rubbed his chin. "Well, if that don't beat all." He chuckled. "You tell 'im ol' Stuart Smith said howdy."

"Yes, sir," the sergeant said. "I will." He extended his hand. "You and the boy take care of yourselves, now." Charlie jumped off the fence and stood at attention. The sergeant smiled and returned his salute. "At ease, soldier," he said, chuckling. Holding the horn of his saddle, the sergeant hesitated a moment before mounting, looking down at Charlie thoughtfully. An idea seemed to strike him.

16

"Maybe when this boy gets a little older, he can ride along and help us drive the cattle up to the fort," the sergeant said. Then with a nod he mounted his horse and rode over to join his men.

Charlie had watched the dust of the trail billow behind the knot of cattle and cavalrymen, and he had felt a frivolous excitement. But that was three weeks ago. He'd just been a child then. Life had become more serious now. A cattle drive might be something he'd have to give some real consideration. Selling beef to the army brought in a reasonable amount of money for him and Gramps. But what if he had to start fending for the two of them, alone?

Charlie finished digging at splinters and cleaned his hands the best he could. They felt stiff, angry, and unremorseful. He hadn't protected them earlier, and they wouldn't shield him from pain now. He guessed that was fair. He'd have to grin and bear it. He tried bending his fingers but couldn't move them much without it hurting a lot and pulling at the blisters. These hands wouldn't do him much good today.

3

CHARLIE ATE A CUP OF RABBIT STEW, then he ladled some of the brown broth into another cup and took it into the bedroom. The gray head of the old man rested on the pillow and his mouth was open. Charlie sat on the chair beside the bed. The room was silent except for the sound of his grandpa's shallow breathing.

"Hi, Gramps. I had my supper; now it's time for you to eat yours," Charlie said, but there was no answer.

The boy clumsily began spooning drops of the lukewarm liquid into his grandpa's mouth. He often had to chase a drop with a ragged napkin as it dribbled down the old, bronzed chin.

Then Charlie just sat there watching his grandpa sleep. *Stuart Smith.* Charlie liked that name. It sounded distinguished and respectable, which fit his grandpa. He was a lanky man, over six feet tall. People often described him as "thin around the waist, but broad in the smile." His gray hair framed keen brown eyes and high cheekbones that rolled down to a square jaw on which rested his famous smile. He proudly claimed his Cherokee blood from his grandmother's side, and he honored that heritage by training himself to be an expert hunter.

Gramps was strong and worked hard maintaining fences and fields, herding, branding and feeding cattle, cutting and splitting firewood, repairing buildings and tools. But his strong arms also knew how to give gentle hugs that assured Chrlie he was never alone in this empty, friendless land. Charlie closed his eyes and imagined Gramps ruffling his hair, as he often did.

"Come back, Gramps." Charlie choked back tears.

The spoon clanked inside the empty cup as Charlie sat it on the bedside table. He couldn't stand the silence, so he filled it with talk. "Fixed seven of them rotten rails in the corral fence today, Gramps," he said. "It was a hassle, but now the cows'll be safe and secure." He looked at his grandpa, hoping for some response, but there wasn't any.

"The fat robin that was hoppin' through the yard all summer's nestled high up in a tree now, waitin' it out for spring. I guess she heard it's gonna be a cold winter, but right now ev'rythin's still as colorful as it was in May, despite the weather that's comin' in. And the chickens are wantin' to stay inside more, too. I gathered ten eggs this mornin', though. Can you believe that, Gramps? The hens are suppose to stop layin' so much this time of year, but I guess this is sorta like their last hurrah. You gotta hurry up an' get better 'cause I can't eat all them eggs by myself."

He giggled, but in the gloomy room his laughter

sounded hollow. The boy didn't mention his blistered hands or his bruised legs, his worries about the dwindling woodpile, or how he lay awake at night shuddering at the wailings of the wind.

He watched his grandpa's chest heave up and down. Then he slowly slid off the chair to the wood floor. How long had it been since Gramps fell sick? Seemed like ages. One day he was fine, laughing and working as usual, and the next day he was complaining of a headache and running a fever. Then for several days he had lain on his bed taking in large gulps of air. One morning he simply fell asleep. Charlie knew he hadn't died, because he could still hear the rasping sound coming from his chest. But he was gone all the same.

"G'night, Gramps," he whispered.

The guttural, labored breaths bothered Charlie, but he didn't know what to do. Bandages wouldn't help. He softly brushed a lock of hair from his grandpa's face, then tucked an extra quilt over him. Then he grabbed the empty soup cup, blew out the lamp, and returned to the main room of the cabin.

Exhausted, but too afraid to sleep, he sat on the floor and stared into the dying fire. "How much longer will Gramps be out?" he asked himself. He didn't know if it was the chill of the evening air or a response to the question, but he shivered. Pulling a blanket from his bedroll, he wrapped it around himself and watched the red embers slowly turn black. There were only a few pieces of firewood left.

Reluctantly he reached for another log, but he moved

too quickly and raked his fingers against the rough bark. Several blisters split open. Darts of pain pierced his fingers as he tossed the log onto the grate and ran to the basin. "Eee-yow," he yelped. He sank his hands into the cool water and moaned. The swollen appendages barely fit into the bowl. "They're a mess," he admitted.

He scooped up some water and let the coolness trickle between the burning fingers and across the palm. He took turns, letting the water soak the hurt from one hand and then do the same for the other. When he was done, he shook his hands with care, but didn't dry them, not wanting to rub them against anything else.

He went to the kitchen window and folded his arms on the sill and looked out into the darkness. The rain storm had passed, leaving a clear, crisp night in its wake. Stars twinkled like ice crystals against the black velvet. The large, round moon smiled down at the cabin with a cheerful glow, scattering pools of light across the valley. How could it look so peaceful, so secure when he felt so lost and uncertain?

"God, if'n you can hear me, help me be strong like Gramps," he whispered. "I'm tryin' hard not to be scared, but I just don't know what to do, with winter comin' an' all. Will you please bring Gramps back to me, God?"

With tired eyes he explored the starry sky, seeking a sign, searching for an answer. But no sign followed; the beautiful emptiness offered no reply to his prayer. Except for an occasional crackle from the fire, all was silent. He turned away from the window and looked down at the floor. "Didn't think I'd get an answer," he mumbled.

Grimacing, he tossed another log onto the grate. He had enough wood for a couple more nights. Soon— tomorrow—he'd have to face his worst fear of all. Gingerly he took the poker and stirred the fire. The embers glowed orange then leapt up onto the logs, eventually spreading into a multi-colored fan of heat. Satisfied the fire would last the night, he pulled his bedroll close to the glow and eased himself between the blankets and comforter.

4

THE THICK, QUILTED COMFORTER HAD been made by Charlie's grandma a few years back. He absentmindedly pulled at its yarn ties, wishing Grandma were still here. Then a sudden, howling wind rushed from the prairie and up against the trees, and Charlie yanked the comforter clear over his head and held his breath in the darkness. A few moments later he brought it back under his chin so he could check on the fire. A gust of cold air whooshed down the chimney and the flames flickered. Briefly, the fire retreated, reminding the boy of the inevitable. Nature was sending him her last warnings. In a couple days there'd be no life or warmth left in that fireplace.

Each day brought winter closer. Ice had begun to etch intricate designs on the cabin windows, glistening in the moonlight. It wouldn't be long now before a blanket of snow would blend the hills and prairie, a feat the wind could never accomplish. That thought gave Charlie a perverse sense of satisfaction. He hated the wind.

Just then, another gust hit the front of the cabin, rattling the doors and windows like an intruder demanding entrance. Clutching the blankets, he watched the fire flicker and fight for survival. "Don't go out," he pleaded. The flames eventually pushed the wind aside and glowed triumphantly, if humbly.

"Gotta get the woodpile stocked, Charlie," he told himself. "Winter's comin' an' you can't fail. If'n you fail, you and Gramps will die, that's all there is to it."

Then from deep within, Charlie heard, "Failure's not an option, son." How many times had he heard his grandpa utter those words but never appreciated their meaning? Failure to kill a squirrel was not a threat, because Gramps always had meat in the stockpot. Failure to gather enough kindling was no threat either, because he always had the woodpile full and ready. But now, to fail at anything was to fail at everything.

Chopping wood scared him more than anything else he had to do because to fail at that meant no fire for food or warmth, and no fire meant death. He knew how to hunt, he knew how to fish, and he could clean and cook whatever he caught or killed. But he didn't know how to swing an ax. The boy let out a heavy sigh and closed his eyes, but as exhausted as he was, sleep would prove to be a negligent friend.

He pushed himself farther down into the puffy folds of his bedroll and tried to relax. His eyelids grew heavy. Then he heard a tap at the front door. Unsure, he opened one eye and looked. Then he heard it again. *Tap, tap.*

"What was that?" he whispered, and his eyes opened wide, searching frantically for an answer. He sat up and listened for another sound, any sound.

Waiting, he strained to hear the scratchy tap again, but after several minutes, he gave up. Hearing nothing but the rude wind, he lowered himself back into his warm blankets.

Then, *tap, tap, tap*. There it was again.

Charlie pulled the covers higher. Who could be out there? "Indians," he whispered. "Maybe it's Indians." The sergeant had told Gramps that since the Sand Creek Massacre some of the Cheyenne had been on the warpath. Charlie had seen a couple of Indian braves when he was in Pueblo with Gramps one time. They were coming out of the X-10-U-8 Saloon, their brightly-colored blankets wrapped around their shoulders. They didn't look like they'd hurt anyone, but then he didn't really know. Maybe this was a rebel Indian.

Again the scratchy tap sounded at the door, this time a little louder and more insistent. Charlie's heart raced. He lay wide-eyed in the darkness, listening to the howling wind, the labored sound of Gramps' breathing coming from the other room, and the scratches at the door. "Go away. Please go away," Charlie whimpered. He pulled the comforter over his head again to drown out all the sounds. Finally, in spite of his fear, a fitful sleep overtook him. And he dreamed.

5

WAIT A MINUTE. CHARLIE TRIED TO THINK. *What'd Gramps just say?* Charlie slowly lowered the rifle to his side. *Did I hear 'im right?* His grandpa's words kept shaping themselves in Charlie's head, re-forming the command he'd just heard, or thought he'd heard, but then they'd tumble into a pile of questions. *Did Gramps say to bring the sight up and aim?* The command was simple but confusing. Gramps had never gone this far with his lesson, usually reclaiming the gun long before this.

The sun beat on his back and the breeze ruffled his hair as he knelt in the tall green grass on the hillside. There in the middle of his lesson, the boy teetered between two choices: acting with uncertainty or questioning his grandpa's instruction. He knew full well neither choice was acceptable, which made the matter worse. He threw a quick glance at his instructor, searching the weathered face for affirmation. To his relief, Gramps gave a sure nod of approval, then grinned slowly and broadly.

26

A thrill coursed through Charlie's body from his head clear down to his fingertips and toes. This wasn't practice! This was a real hunt and Gramps was going to let him shoot his big gun. After years of lessons, Gramps must've finally realized that Charlie was a man, albeit a small one, one who could be entrusted with his most-prized and powerful possession. Charlie was overwhelmed with excitement, but now was not the time to give in to his feelings. Now was the time to hunt and prove to Gramps that he'd made a wise decision. Charlie swallowed hard then inhaled deeply, pulling air far down into his lungs, harnessing his emotions. *Hold it back till later*, he commanded himself.

Completely focused now, the boy's eyes searched from tree to tree for what Gramps had already seen, as his own eyes adjusted to the various shades of the pine forest. Finally, among the mottled shadows, there was revealed the contrasting color and shape of a large animal's beige coat. Charlie rested his sight on the target. Words from lessons past beat in his ears, "Failure is not an option, son." Well, he wouldn't fail, he'd see to that.

He watched the deer under the tree and his breathing quickened, sending cold beads of sweat down the back of his neck and under his shirt. Excitement raced through every vein. The breeze chilled his damp skin. He shivered. The smell of pine mingled with that of the damp earth and heightened the musk of his own sweat. These, along with the full outline of the doe, brought his nerves to the edge and sent erratic impulses through his system. But he refused to lose focus, holding tight to all he'd been taught.

27

He wanted to bag this prize for Gramps.

Steadily raising the rifle, he tucked it tight into his shoulder and brought the deer into its sight. Then, without warning the doe raised her head and seemed to look right at him. Gramps held up a finger, signaling him to wait. He knew he had a clear shot, but to disobey Gramps now would mean the end of his lessons, probably forever. So he relaxed the gun and waited.

Seconds slowly passed and his excitement turned to anxiety. The teacher and student knelt side by side, watching the long ears of the mule deer turn and try to hear what her nose had already brought to her attention. Her large, liquid eyes scanned the landscape, searching every shadow, every crevice for danger. Charlie held his breath, hoping the shadows that shielded their bodies from the sun would conceal their position. They dared not move—hardly even breathe—for risk of alerting her to their whereabouts and causing her to dart up the dark hills.

After what seemed like an eternity, the doe lowered her head and resumed nibbling on the dry grass beneath the pine, her ears still alert and listening. Charlie let out a long sigh. Seconds passed. Finally, Gramps nodded.

With firm resolve, Charlie repositioned the gun. The sight, once again squared with the deer's shoulder, targeted the point of entry. "Now, when you're ready," Gramps whispered, "slowly pull back on the trigger." Inhaling deeply, the boy wrapped his forefinger around the big metal hook; exhaling, he gently pulled it back towards his chest.

Boom!

Charlie's body jerked. Taut muscles bolted him upright in his bedroll. Fighting panic, he rubbed his eyes and looked around the cabin. What had happened? The log in the fireplace was still crackling, sending red shards of embers up into the flue with every loud pop. Disappointed, he recognized the truth: it wasn't the boom of the gun that had awakened him, but an exploding log in the fireplace. Staring at the fire in disbelief, Charlie was overcome by a sickening feeling of something lost. "It was only a dream," he whispered. "It was only a dream." Nothing had changed. Gramps was still sleeping and Charlie was still alone. He wanted to scream, but he dared not. Instead, he suffocated the urge by stuffing a corner of the comforter into his mouth and biting down hard.

In the dark cabin Charlie blinked and scanned the room, trying to focus on its familiarity. There was his grandpa's black powder rifle hanging in its usual place above the fireplace mantle. It was a .58 caliber, 1853 Armi Sport Muzzleloader. Grandma had given it to Gramps as a surprise for his 60th birthday. It measured almost five feet from the sparkling brass butt plate to the nose cap and the initials *S.C.S.* were etched into the walnut stock. Charlie squinted at the letters from where he lay. The barrel was a smoky blue-gray. Gramps called it "Big Blue," and he'd been teaching Charlie how to use it so they could hunt big game together. But then Gramps fell ill and the lessons ended.

In real life, Charlie'd never shot the gun. He'd never even considered it. Gramps taught him that Big Blue was a man's gun, too much for a boy, and it would be years before he'd have the privilege of shooting it.

Charlie let his gaze drift down the mountain rocks that formed the face of the chimney and fireplace. There in the shade of the mantle, within easy reach, hung his own Hawken squirrel gun made in St. Louie. It was an old one of Gramps' that he'd given to Charlie two years ago. Charlie used it for target practice and for hunting small game, but it could never be used to kill deer or elk. A familiar lump formed in his throat. "I ain't a man yet, Gramps," he whispered, "but I'm gonna hafta be, because you're sick, and we gotta survive this winter somehow."

Closing his eyes, he bit his quivering lip, fighting the tears, but they came anyway. They trickled from the corners of his brown eyes and flowed down his cheeks, mixing with the dirt that streaked his freckled face, a face that hadn't grinned for some time. He frowned and scolded himself. "Stop crying, Charlie." He rolled over and buried his face in his blankets. The wind moaned the words of its solemn lullaby, "Tomorrow he'll be a man; tonight he's still a boy." He cried himself to sleep.

6

THE SUN'S CHEERFUL, RADIANT FINGERS shed the night's black velvet gloves and wiped the frost from the windows, then chased the dark shadows into secret corners of the cabin. Charlie shivered and remembered his dream. It had been so real! But when he looked up above the fireplace, he saw Big Blue hanging there, where Gramps had left it before he fell into his long sleep.

Then Charlie remembered the tapping at the door he'd heard last night. But nothing in the room was amiss; no rebel Indians had barged into the cabin and killed him and Gramps. The fire was low, but it was still alive and all their possessions were in their usual places. He wriggled out of his bedroll and went to the door. He unlatched it and, with some difficulty, pushed it open and peered outside. Heaped against the door was a pile of dried out tumbleweeds. "Darn ol' tumbleweeds. That's all it was." Things could sure seem different in the night.

It was cold outside. Charlie closed the door and latched

it again. His hands hurt. They felt like they'd been the ones scraping sharp icy shards off of frozen windows. With his fingertips he gingerly tossed a couple of logs on the fire grate.

"I better get the broth for Gramps." He turned and reached toward the soup pot, then out of the corner of his eye he noticed Big Blue again. He stood straight and folded his arms across his chest. A sneaky thought turned itself into rational temptation. "Charlie, the fact is you gotta be the man of this house now, so that gives you permission to shoot Big Blue." He said these words in a matter-of-fact tone. "I mean, what if that'd been a rebel Indian tryin' to get in last night? If'n you'd 'a tried to shoot 'im with your piddly gun, he'd 'a had you and Gramps both scalped, dried, an' hangin' from 'is tomahawk before he'd 'a felt the sting." He kicked a piece of bark under the counter and began to pace the floor. "Blasted tumbleweeds," he continued. "Kept me up half the night frettin' 'bout stuff I don't need to be frettin' 'bout, like Indians an' firewood, an' the silly sound the wind makes."

Charlie's pace quickened. "It's up to you to take care of things 'round here, Charlie," he muttered. "It's too far to walk to the Tuttle's farm. Pueblo is a day's ride from here, and there ain't no one at the schoolhouse this time of year. Besides, Gramps could wake up any minute an' I don't wanna be gallivantin' 'round the prairie lookin' for help and leavin' 'im all alone."

"And besides," he sputtered. "I'm gettin' tired of dried biscuits an' it's time Gramps had some fresh broth. We need us some new meat, and that little gun of yours ain't gonna bring it down. Well, splittin' firewood can wait one more day, the chores can wait one more day, ev'rythin' can wait one more day!"

But how could he even think about putting off the dreaded chore of wood chopping and taking the gun out without his grandpa? Wouldn't that be breaking a trust? Well, if so, Gramps would surely have to understand!

"Nope, you're gonna shoot with Big Blue from now on, learn to fend for this here farm instead of sittin' 'round like some scared girl, like … like Mary Lou Tuttle. Now, there's a scaredy cat for you. Nope, you ain't gonna be 'fraid of ev'rythin' like Mary Lou, you ain't. Things are gonna change 'round here, startin' today."

Grabbing the cup, Charlie filled it with broth, then went in and fed Gramps just as he'd done the last several mornings, but this time he barely spoke.

7

IN THE BARN, CHARLIE PULLED THE STOOL under Nellie and pressed his head against the ribs of the milk cow, trying to find the rhythm of this morning's milking. Within seconds, streams of rich white liquid squirted against the sides of the metal bucket. *Ping, ping!* the sound echoed. Nellie relaxed and Charlie tried to concentrate on his chore, but his thoughts wandered to the adventure that lay ahead.

The milking done, Charlie picked up the heavy pail, absentmindedly sloshing some of the milk over the rim of the bucket. He stopped to check on Bessie. The mare watched him with worried eyes. "I know you an' Gramps been partners a long time, girl," Charlie said. "But there ain't nothin' you can do to help 'im right now." Bessie whinnied in disagreement as Charlie turned and hobbled through the flock of hens that were pecking at the last of the corn he'd tossed on the barnyard for them earlier.

Back in the house, his chores finally finished, he pulled

a chair over to the fireplace and climbed up. He was a little nervous about his decision. He'd never gone anywhere without Gramps, and he'd never used a gun without his permission or assistance. Now he was getting ready to do both.

His blistered hands trembled as he stood on his tiptoes and gently pulled Big Blue down off of its pegs. Stepping to the floor, he laid the gun on the table. He rubbed his fingertips across its smooth stock and traced the carved initials, *S.C.S.* "It's his gun, but Gramps ain't really here to grant permission to use it, so I give you permission, Charlie," he whispered to himself. His mind was made up.

He bustled about the kitchen and gathered what he needed for a hunting trip: black powder, lead balls, cloth strips, his pouch, a knife, and a canteen of water. The last things he threw into his bag were a couple of hard biscuits and some of his grandpa's beef jerky. That would have to do for lunch. As he headed out the door, he turned and looked back into the cabin. The fire softly crackled, beckoning him to stay, but all else was still and dark, offering no such invitation. Closing the door behind him, the small boy tightened his grasp on the big gun and headed up the hill into the shadows of the tall trees.

Several hours passed and Charlie hadn't seen or heard anything worth shooting. If he'd had his own gun, he could've easily bagged a few squirrels and a couple of rabbits, but those were too small for Big Blue, so he let them pass. Once in a while, he spotted deer tracks, but so far, neither doe nor buck had shown itself. Resting on a rock, he leaned the gun within easy reach and wiped the sweat from his forehead with the back of his sleeve. It was a brisk day, but the climb had made him hot, thirsty, and hungry. Searching his bag, he pulled out the jerky, bit off a piece of the flavorful leather and chomped until it began to soften in his mouth.

He looked around and listened. The call of an owl startled him. "Strange," whispered Charlie. "Owls don't usually come out till evenin', but this one must 'a been bothered by somethin'."

A rabbit scurried past his feet and darted into a hole at the base of a tree. A gentle breeze softly fluttered his hair and heightened the scent of the natural elements around him. The ground, still damp from yesterday's rain, smelled sweet, while the evergreens offered their pungent perfume. Looking out over the plains that stretched for miles and miles, Charlie imagined he could see all the way to the Kansas Territory.

Charlie used to play up here, back when times were happier around the cabin. While Gramps would collect pine cones for kindling, Charlie would pretend he was an Indian tracker, hiding behind trees and rocks, following his grandpa undetected—or so he thought. Gramps never let on then, but later he told Charlie he had known where he was every second. He couldn't see him, but he could hear him. Now Charlie chewed on the jerky and smiled at the memories.

He looked across the hills. The blazing aspens decorated the evergreen forest with dollops of gold that could make even the poorest man feel rich. This was home and Charlie loved it.

He was lifting the water canteen to his mouth when, out of the corner of his eye, he saw a sudden movement. A clump of brush about twenty feet away swayed slowly at first, then shook wildly to and fro. He set the canteen down on the rock and kept watching. Then his curiosity got the better of him. He shoved the rest of the jerky into his pocket and got up to investigate. Cautiously he moved towards the brush, listening. Then two bear cubs tumbled out towards him. Startled, he jumped back as the balls of fur bounded past him. He laughed nervously and watched the cubs roll and wrestle a few yards from his feet.

"Why, you're just little things," he said. "Prob'ly just a few months old. Tryin' to run some of that energy off before you take your winter nap, huh fellas?" He spoke loudly, trying to slow the pace of his pounding heart with the sound of his own voice. The cubs ignored him and romped on through the timber, tumbling down a gentle slope as each tested the other's strength. He smiled and watched a moment longer and then headed back to the rock.

A sharp cry made him spin on his heels. One of the cubs was standing on its hind legs, pawing at the air and bawling in pain. Its sibling offered no comfort, but ignored the cries for help, finding interest in a berry bush instead. Alarmed, Charlie thought it best to quickly gather his belongings and move on. The boy slung his bag over his shoulder and picked up the gun, when another movement in the brush made him stop in his tracks. At first he thought the breeze was playing tricks on him, but then reality snapped into focus. Watching the cubs, he'd forgotten that their mother would definitely be somewhere in close proximity. Too close.

Hearing her cub cry, the golden grizzly had reared to her full height of seven feet. She was only about fifty feet away when she and Charlie spotted each other. According to her, he was an obstacle, or even a threat, standing between her and her babies. Her senses told her that this stranger was the reason her cub was bawling, and she let out a deafening roar. Charlie dropped what he was holding and shielded his ears with his hands. Paralyzed with fear, his eyes searched for a place to hide, a place of safety, as the bear continued her warning roar.

His brain demanded a plan and commanded his eyes to search quickly. Scouring the hillside, he noticed a small enclave of aspen forming a tight circle in front of an outcropping of rock. It was a natural haven offering temporary safety and it was all he had; he was out of time.

The cub bawled again and the bear charged. Charlie could hear her tearing through the brush, coming up fast behind him. His heart hammered against his chest wall. His brain ordered his legs to move. The bear bounded closer and he bolted toward the clump of trees. Focused on reaching the shelter, he didn't care what he lost at that moment, as long as it wasn't his life. His only hope was to reach those trees in time.

Charlie struggled up the incline, his legs cramping as he dug his toes into the wet, mossy slope of the hill. She was getting closer. He could hear her panting grunts as she climbed up behind him. For some reason, he remembered the jerky in his pocket. He pulled it out and threw it as far off to the side as he could, hoping it would distract her, if only for a second. He groped up the hill. He was almost there. But he was out of breath and weak. He felt her bearing down on him, but he couldn't look back. Time was too precious.

Instinctively he closed his eyes and dove toward the fortress. Landing within inches of the trees, he scrambled on his belly. In desperation, he pulled himself up and pushed his body between the tightly knit trunks of the trees. The bear, ignoring the jerky, lunged forward. With one swipe of her powerful paw, her claws ripped through the back of Charlie's pants, shredding the flesh just as he pulled his leg into the confines of his sanctuary.

Angry that he'd escaped, the grizzly reared to her hind legs again, threw her magnificent head back, and roared, telling all who cared to hear that the boy was doomed. Sobbing, he fell back against the rock. "Leave me alone," he screamed. "I didn't do nothin'!" The bear paid no attention to her captive's pleas, but kept bellowing out her warning.

Charlie fell to the ground and pulled his knees to his chest. Wrapping his arms tightly around them, he formed a ball with his body. He peered at her from underneath his arm as she tore at the tree trunks with her claws, ferociously thrashing and biting them with her long, sharp teeth. He shook and cried uncontrollably.

Taking the white trunk of an aspen with her claws,

she forced it to bend, pulling it to the ground with extraordinary strength. Charlie held his breath as he watched, relieved that despite her fierce determination, the tree didn't break. Moving on to a smaller tree, she tried again. She bent the sapling to the ground, shredding it to pieces as she desperately tried to reach him, only to find the entrance of his protective circle restricted by larger and stronger trees that shielded the boy from certain death.

Dust, leaves, tree limbs and dirt flew in all directions as her rage intensified. He knew she was determined to kill him, but he had nowhere else to go. Even if by some miracle he were to survive the attack, his pant leg was soaked with blood and he feared he would die one way or the other. Seething hatred flowed from her eyes. Watching her, he concluded that miracles weren't real, not for him anyway.

Wishing he could close his eyes and lose her in the darkness that kept tugging at his senses, the boy heard both cubs screaming now, somewhere in the distance. The bear, snorting and huffing, stopped her rampage for just a moment and listened. She didn't turn from glaring at Charlie with blazing eyes between the wooden pillars, or blasting him with hot, putrid breath from her gaping mouth. Foam, mixed with crushed leaves and dirt, oozed between her teeth and spilled onto the grassy floor.

Her lips rolled back, baring yellow fangs. Her panting quickened. Their eyes met and she glared at the enemy. With every breath she seemed to whisper her murderous intent to kill him. Charlie trembled, knowing she was poised to resume the attack. Then once again the cubs' cries splintered the air. Throwing a last angry glance at the boy, the bear spun around and raced down the embankment towards her cubs, sending a torrent of dust and leaves spiraling upward with every step. As suddenly as she'd attacked, she was gone.

Charlie sat still and listened, but didn't dare move. Where had she gone? Would she come back? Should he run? The questions floated away unanswered. He tried to decide what to do. At first there was only silence, but within seconds, blood-curdling screams pierced the air. The wild animal that had dared to disturb the cubs was now receiving the mother's full wrath. She was determined to kill something, and by the sound of it, the perpetrator, innocent or not, had no hope of escape.

It was almost too much for Charlie. He wanted to stay curled up beneath the swaying branches, to forget about everything, to escape into the terror and shock that threatened his very sanity. But, instead, with trembling fingers he tied pieces of his ripped pants around his leg to stop the bleeding. Tears and sweat rolled down his face as he slowly crept out of the trees. Fearing the fight would soon end and the bear would return for him, he didn't linger or look back. All he wanted to do was get to the cabin and close the door behind him. Breathless, he cut a wide swath around the nightmarish sounds of the fighting animals as he dragged his wounded leg down the hill toward the safety of home.

PUSHING THROUGH SHRUBS AND ROCKS, Charlie struggled down the hillside. Minutes seemed like hours as he fought the urge to surrender to the enclosing darkness and the clouds that kept filling his head. Finally he saw the cabin rising like a ghostly mirage above the prairie. He couldn't hear the fight anymore. But the bear's angry growl and the screams of agony still echoed in his ears. He flung himself through the back door and onto the kitchen floor. Kicking the door closed with his good leg, he lay there numb, shivering and sweating, reliving the nightmare over and over. With the last of his strength he reached for his bedroll and pulled a blanket over his chilled, shaking form.

The cabin was silent except for his grandpa's deep-sleep breathing. He longed to hear a human voice. In a delirium of fear and shock, his feverish thoughts returned to the comment he'd made earlier about Mary Lou Tuttle. "I ain't got no business callin' you a scaredy cat, Mary Lou," he said as he lay shivering on the cabin floor. "And I ain't never gonna try to scare you again, I promise."

As if in a dream he saw Mary Lou, the little sister of his best friend, Wilbur. He remembered how her brown hair had shone in the sunshine that fall day when he had last seen his friends. Her pigtails were tied with blue ribbons. Charlie and Wilbur chased her with a beetle and a snake, then laughed as she screamed and ran to her mother.

"You prob'ly weren't never alone at night with wind rat-tlin' the door, Mary Lou, or had a bear that wanted you dead." He groaned and continued. "I ain't never been so scared in all my life. I shoulda walked to the Tuttle farm when Gramps got sick. I shoulda gone for help somehow, when I coulda."

If he'd done that, Charlie might have been there with the Tuttles right now, in their warm farmhouse, helping Wilbur with his everyday chores and eating Mrs. Tuttle's chicken 'n dumplings and cornbread. Mr. Tuttle would be taking care of all the big things like repairing fences and … splitting firewood. *Wilbur doesn't hafta do any of that. And he doesn't hafta worry 'bout keepin' his grandpa alive, either.*

Charlie's heart was still beating fast and he was panting. His mind was in a fog. He felt like he was in some strange dream, seeing pictures come and go before his eyes. The last time he saw the Tuttles … When was it? A few months ago? Charlie wasn't sure. The weather had been warm. There was a visiting preacher at the church—an evangelist, they called him. Not the usual once-a-month circuit preacher. Gramps had hitched Bessie to the wagon, and the two of them had eaten a quick breakfast, done morning chores, dressed in their Sunday best, and headed out before sunrise. It seemed so long ago. Back when he was a kid and life was so simple and Gramps was always there.

Charlie's mind wouldn't stop racing and the memories of that day all blurred together. Wilbur in the second row with his ma, pa, two older brothers, and Mary Lou. Charlie and Gramps in the back row. Everyone singing "I am Bound for the Promised Land." Someone playing harmonica. Someone else playing fiddle. Mary Lou slowly turning her head and sticking out her tongue. Charlie crossing his eyes at her. Mrs. Tuttle whispering something in Mary Lou's ear that made her turn around and sit up straight.

The preacher with sweat rolling down his red face, pacing the front of the room, waving a Bible in one hand, and punctuating the air with his other hand. Words. Lots of words about the fiery flames of Hell. Men shouting "Amen." Women trying to keep the babies quiet. The preacher talking about Heaven then, in a lower, calmer voice, but still with intense firey eyes, like he was seeing that beautiful place right in front of him and all the dead saints there, living.

Charlie's leg was bleeding and the pictures in his mind started fading as unconsciousness threatened. But he struggled against it and tried to remember. That day after church, people were there from all the farms around, everyone eating a potluck picnic on the grass. There were tables with bright cloths. And basket after basket of food carried from wagons—baked beans, fried chicken, potato salad, pies, cakes, and buckets of milk and water. The edges of the table linens waved in the breeze like flags.

The children were running and playing, eager for the blessing to be said. Charlie and Gramps had to get back home before dark. But the days were longer then. Mr. Tuttle gave the children the last watermelon from his field. They had a seed-spitting contest and Wilbur won. He always won. Then they played in the grasses and wildflowers and the grown-ups sat in the shade.

Charlie could feel the darkness starting to overtake him. But he kept fighting against it. He remembered Wilbur hiding his face in his arm and leaning against a tree, counting to twenty while the others found places to hide. Charlie jumped behind the fallen tree trunk at the same time Mary Lou jumped in from another direction. Mary Lou tossed her pigtails and grinned at him with such a sparkle in her blue eyes that it startled him and he jumped up and ran to the corral and ducked behind the water trough. Then Wilbur called "all in free." Mary Lou laughed when Charlie fell off the fence, scrambling to get back to home base.

Then Charlie and Gramps were riding home, long and silent, each thinking his own thoughts. Charlie was trying to imagine what it'd be like with a complete family, a mother and father and sisters and brothers as well as grandparents.

The wagon creaked as the wheels rolled in the deep ruts of the road. The sun flashed through the treetops, casting long evening shadows. Gramps leaned forward with his elbows on his knees and held Bessie's reigns loosely in his fingers. His wide-brimmed hat hung low over his eyes. He started singing one of his favorite hymns.

> Unto the hills I lift my eye;
> Your promised aid I claim:
> Father of mercies, glorify
> Your son, dear Jesus' name.
> Salvation in that name is found,
> Balm of my grief and care;
> A medicine for every wound,—
> All, all I want is there.

"Gramps?" Charlie had interrupted him. "I liked that new song the 'vangelist taught us today. Could we sing that song?" Charlie thought the hymns his grandpa sang were ancient and kind of hard to follow. The new song had a catchier tune and the words were easier.

"I'll try, son, if you get it started."

Charlie remembered the tune and between him and Gramps, they recalled most of the words.

> My hope is built on nothing less
> Than Jesus' blood and righteousness;
> I dare not trust the sweetest frame,
> But wholly lean on Jesus' name.

"Gramps?" Charlie had another question.

"What now, Charlie?"

"I been wonderin'. You know what the preacher said

'bout Heaven? Well … is that where Grandma is now? And my pa and ma, too?"

Gramps kept his eyes on the road. "I believe so."

"I know Grandma got sick an' God took 'er to Heaven, but why'd my ma and pa hafta go?" Gramps didn't offer a reason, but started humming the first hymn again.

That day seemed a long time ago. Now Charlie lay on the cabin floor shaking violently. His breathing was quick and shallow. *I'm gonna die too, right here*, he thought. He wished he'd asked Gramps a lot more questions.

What happened to Ma when I was born? How come I lived and she didn't? Why doesn't anyone talk about it?

The cabin seemed to sway. Charlie felt dizzy. And sick. And there was no one he could call out to. He was alone. And he had failed. "Stop dreamin', Charlie. You ain't at the Tuttles, and Mary Lou wouldn't smile at you now if she knew what you just did." The words bubbled to the surface as he choked on his tears. "There's no one close by who can hear you, and you ain't even close to Heaven. And you failed bad. Real bad."

Not bringing back any game, wasting the day, losing all his stuff … "Failure's not an option, Gramps," he mumbled through chattering teeth. "So by doin' what I did—losin' Big Blue, gettin' hurt, I've done worse than fail you. I've kilt you—kilt both of us, because now I got no one."

Even God had deserted him. Why? Hot, angry tears puddled in the corners of his eyes and spilled down his cheeks as the shadows rushed his mind, extinguishing the light of consciousness.

47

9

THE WIND WHISTLED AND RACED ROUND the corners of the cabin, pushing forward the cold breath of approaching snow. Charlie shuddered and slowly opened his eyes. The cabin was completely dark: no lamps, no fire, no light of any kind. He lay for a moment trying to remember where he was and what had happened. He was cold, cold to the core, deathly cold. Within moments, the silhouette of the fireplace emerged from the darkness. Its cavernous mouth seemed to be calling to him, but the words made no sense to his numb mind. He closed his eyes again and let his head sink back into the soft folds of his blanket.

Another gust of wind rattled the door. Like flowing water, cold air pushed in under the door and fanned across the wooden floor, engulfing Charlie's twitching body. The blast pulled at his consciousness. His eyes opened wide and he understood the message of the fireplace.

I gotta get up and restart the fire or we'll freeze, he thought. Throwing the blanket aside, he sat up, but he moved too fast. Searing arcs of pain ran up his legs and through his body, grabbing at his breath.

Convulsing, he tried to gain control, but of what, he wasn't sure. When he stopped fighting and relaxed his muscles, the pain began to subside in waves. Each breath released a bit of its grip but opened the door to his memory, allowing everything to flood back into his mind: the cubs, the bear, the gun ... everything.

He pulled his knees to his chest. He glanced above the mantle, but the pegs were barren. "I lost the gun," he moaned. "I lost Big Blue. I lost my grandpa's gun."

Panic gripped him. "Gramps!" he whispered. "How long've I been layin' here? Who took care of Gramps?" This time he slowly forced himself up, wrestling with the pain through gritted teeth. His leg was fevered and swollen, screaming in torture. His hands were bruised and stiff and his head felt as if it would split in two. The rest of his body was just plain sore. But none of that mattered now. Gritting his teeth, he grabbed a chair and pulled himself to his feet.

Limping over to the remnants of logs left in the wood bin, he counted. "One, two, three, four, five. If I stretch it, I can get two days," he muttered. "What was I thinkin'?" Pushing the lecture aside for later, he limped to the fireplace and felt the iron kettle. The bottom was warm, as were the cinders that lay below it on the fireplace floor. "I musta been out 'bout a day," he mumbled. "Lordy, I hope Gramps is okay." He tried to move quickly, but he was weak and his wracked limbs slowed his pace. What used to be a simple task, now took several laborious minutes. Despite his strained movements, a fire roared to life, filling the cabin with precious warmth. He got a cup, and taking a moment to steady his hands, he carefully ladled some broth then limped into the bedroom.

He set the cup down. Then, with dread, he lit a wooden match and touched it to the cloth wick of the oil lamp. It caught immediately, and soon a small flame was casting shadows that danced about the small room. Charlie went over and laid his head on his grandpa's chest. There was a faint heartbeat. The boy raised up and gazed at the withered old man who looked nothing like he remembered. "I'm sorry, Gramps," he cried softly. "I'm sorry I almost kilt you." Unable to contain the tears any longer, Charlie buried his face in his hands and wept bitterly.

No warm arms engulfed him. Only cold wisps of air encircled his shoulders as the northern wind invaded the cracks of the timber walls. Would someone, something hear the pleas that poured from his heart? "Please, dear God," he whispered hoarsely, "please help Gramps. He's dyin' and I can't save 'im. Please help." Burying his face in his grandpa's chest, he cried again.

Charlie rubbed his eyes and left streaks of dirt across his red cheeks. The salty tears bit at his blisters, but he didn't care. Taking the cup from the table, he leaned close to Gramps and began to patiently slide the spoon between the shriveled, chapped, ashen lips. Silently he prayed his efforts wouldn't be in vain.

By reflex Gramps swallowed every spoonful until the cup was empty. Through his shudders, Charlie whispered,

"I didn't mean to fail you, Gramps. I'm sorry. With all my heart, I'm sorry. If'n you stay, I'll make it up to you, I promise. I'll be a man to make you proud … if'n you just stay, Gramps."

Charlie became aware that his leg was throbbing. Grimacing with each painful step, he limped back into the kitchen and pulled a small pot from the cupboard. For a quick boil, he filled it halfway with water and hung it directly above the fire, then grabbed a clean rag and slid down onto the floor. Very slowly, he pulled the encrusted remnants of his pants from his leg, careful not to open any of the lacerations left by the grizzly. Caked in dried blood, five deep wounds ran across the back of his left calf. From what he could see, the bear hadn't raked her claws far enough down to expose the bone, but the wounds were deep enough that they should've been sewed shut for proper healing. He knew he couldn't do that, so he settled for a thorough cleaning of the gashes.

Dipping the cloth into the hot water, he slowly began to dab and wipe away the crimson crust, cringing as the fevered wounds pounded with pain. He bit his lip and forced himself to finish the task. When he was satisfied that he had cleaned them well, he leaned against a chair and rested. "That was the easy part," he admitted. "The hardest part is comin' next."

Charlie sucked in a mouthful of air and pulled himself up, wrestling with the pain just as before. He wiped the sweat from his brow and limped to the cupboard, searching out the bottle of whiskey his grandpa kept for situations like this. Drinking alcohol was frowned upon in the Smith family, but using it to clean open wounds was definitely permitted. He'd seen Gramps use it once when he'd cut his hand while gutting an elk. Gramps had told him, "Whiskey sets things right when used as medicine, but never did no good when used as a drink."

Yanking the cork out of the bottle with his teeth, he placed his bent knee on a chair. He looked over his shoulder at the wounds. From that angle, he saw the black and blue streaks that ran from the gashes and disappeared under his pant leg. It reminded him of the map hanging on the wall down at the schoolhouse. The thought made him chuckle bitterly. *It'd be a map all right*, he thought. *A map showing where not to go.*

Charlie spit the cork onto the table. He took a wooden spoon and clenched the handle between his teeth. Steadying himself with one hand, he held the whiskey bottle with the other and poured the golden liquid over each gash. His breath stopped. His hands shook. Never had he felt anything like this. He closed his eyes tightly and imagined the red hot pokers that were being thrust into the wounds and ripping through his leg. He sat the bottle down on the counter with a thud and sank his teeth into the wooden handle. He let out low, guttural noises as waves of nausea rolled over him. Then, before he could think about it, he grabbed the bottle again with trembling hands and sloshed the golden medicine across the shredded muscle again.

His sweat-soaked hair was matted to his head, his shirt clung to his back, and the bottle was nearly empty when he sat it back down on the counter. "It's clean, Charlie," he said, panting. He collapsed upon the table and waited for his innards to quiet down. Salty sweat stung his eyes. But his nerves started easing back from the brink. Finally, he pushed himself away from the table, grabbed two biscuits from the basket, and limped over to his bedroll. Not bothering to smooth out the blankets, he eased himself down and rested his head on their folds, but before he could finish draping a blanket over his legs, he fell into an exhausted sleep. The two hard biscuits fell from his swollen fingers and rolled onto the cabin floor.

The next day was cold and dark, sleeting at times. A thin coat of ice covered the desolate ground. Charlie was stiff and sore, barely able to walk. All he could do was rest, doctor his wounds, and tend to his grandpa.

He fed Gramps small portions of broth several times during the day and doubled his water intake. Before dusk, the parched lips began to soften. By evening, Gramps had regained some of his normal color, not quite so gray.

Little pellets of ice hit the cabin roof as Charlie limped over to the firewood and stared gloomily at the remaining three fragments of wood. Tomorrow was the day, come hail or high water. He picked up the largest of the three pieces and threw it onto the grate. The fire would last through the night with the remaining wood, but then tomorrow both the fire and its fuel would be gone. "Tomorrow," he said, sighing.

10

THE NEXT MORNING, THE WOODPILE was waiting, but first Charlie had to make sure all the animals could get to their water. Everything was coated with a thin layer of ice. One by one, he went from trough to pan and chipped the crust away so the cows in the field, the animals in the barn, and the chickens in the coop could drink. This was the first time he'd been outside since the bear attack, but he didn't have time to worry about *her* right now. He was going to have a hard enough time handling this situation without having to continually look over his shoulder.

Charlie was already tired, but he couldn't rest yet. Nellie needed milking something terrible. She let him know about it the minute he stepped into the barn. Her mournful scolding echoed through the rafters as he gathered the stool and the pail. As soon as he started milking her, she stopped her bawling. "Sorry, Nellie," he whispered. "I just couldn't move yesterday." She relaxed at the sound of his voice and let the milk flow, but would cast a watchful eye at him occasionally, suspecting he'd try to finish before she was ready. To her relief, albeit painful to his hands, he finished the chore, taking considerably more time than normal.

He tossed a bundle of clean hay to Bessie and then scooped a handful of corn for the chickens. On his way back from the barn, he blew his warm breath into the frigid morning air, and steam swirled in front of his face. He was mentally preparing himself for the next challenge.

He looked beyond the wood-chopping stump and the fat logs that lay around it, and tried to turn his attention, instead, to the neglected garden that lay just beyond. For a moment he was tempted to get the hoe and try digging up potatoes, but he knew he had something much more important that needed doing. He looked back at the stump. The waiting ax leaned against it. Charlie knew he had to at least try.

Before Gramps got sick he'd been cutting down deadwood and getting ready to split those large pieces into fire logs. Now, straightening his hat, Charlie picked up a log and set it on the stump. He grabbed the ax and looked up and down the long handle and felt the heavy head. "Nothin' to it," muttered the boy. "Big Blue was heavier than this." Grasping the handle, he lined up the head with the intended target and drew a deep breath. "You can do this, Charlie," he mumbled. His own encouragement sounded weak, but he raised the ax high over his head. To his surprise, the weight of the iron rocked him back and forth. Fighting to keep his balance, he brought the ax down with all the might he could muster, but it hit loose, barely scratching the log.

Splitting firewood definitely wasn't as easy as Gramps made it look, but then his grandpa was a big man. And he didn't have to work with monstrous, stinging fingers. To add to the challenge, the ax handle was almost as tall as Charlie was, so swinging it over his head made balancing himself almost impossible. Determined to find a stance that would give him the advantage, he planted his feet firmly on the ground and again pulled the ax up and over, cringing as he felt the wooden handle tear at his hands through his grandpa's work gloves.

He concentrated hard on his balance, but to no avail. When he brought the ax down, the thrust threw him forward, the blade only nicking the log. Chips flew everywhere and the log bounced off the stump onto the icy ground. Trying it again and again proved futile. The ground took several blows, but the log was always left intact. After each determined blow, he would stand up straight and either find the log still perched on the stump, looking at him like a stubborn bird, or lying on the ground—but either way, it was intact. Exhausted, he stumbled over to the well, intending to rinse the sweat from his face.

"More ice," he grumbled as he looked down the stone shaft. Charlie lowered the bucket and tapped it on the frosty coating several times until he heard the crackling sound of breaking ice. He pulled the bucket back up until it dangled a couple of feet above the ice and then let it fall with a thud. After several tries, the ice gave way. Staring into the icy water, he saw what should have been his reflection, but he didn't recognize the thin, pale boy that stared back through the small chunks of bobbing ice. "I ain't gonna cry," he whispered. "There's no one to do this but me, so I'll figure it out somehow."

He'd forgotten why he'd come to the well. Grasping the ax handle as if it were the arm of an unruly child, he tromped back over to the stump, pulled off the gloves and threw them to the ground. Determined, he concentrated on his target as he brought the ax up high and swung it downward. But all he did was knock the wood from its perch and plunge the blade into the stump. It took him a few minutes to free the ax head, but when he did, he hammered relentlessly at the logs, determined more than ever to master this chore. After all, he'd fixed the fence, milked the cow, hunted for game, and kept both himself and his grandpa alive. Surely, he could learn to chop wood. About mid-day, he stepped back to take inventory of his efforts. To his dismay, most of the wood had been split into slivers and chunks that weren't fit for anything except kindling.

Done in, he fell to his knees. Sharp arrows of pain pierced his leg, ripping open two of the gashes that had begun to mend. Kneeling there, he could feel the warm fluid ooze out and mix with the cloth of his pants. His hands were bleeding too—all signs of healing gone as old blisters gave birth to larger, more excruciating sores. After a half-day, this was all he had to show for his efforts. Charlie let his chin drop to his chest. "I failed again," he groaned.

The prairie wind picked itself up and hurled bits of ice

across the grass. Twirling up into the hills, it teased the ice-coated Indian summer blooms and began to sweep away the last colors of fall. Charlie was defeated. He squeezed his eyes closed. The wind blew ice into his face, stinging his cheeks. "God, help me," he whispered.

Flakes of snow caught on his lashes as he painfully rose to his feet. But it was reality, not merely the weather, that chilled him to the bone. Winter was here; he was out of time. "Gramps said failure's not an option, so I'll give it one more try." He took the ax and started to raise it over his head.

Just then he heard the sound of horse hooves galloping across the high, frozen prairie. Someone was coming, but who could it be? He lowered the ax to the ground. Why would anyone want to venture out on such a cold, gray day? Charlie hesitated for a second. Maybe it was an outlaw making his escape, or maybe it was a neighbor who needed his help. Either way, it was up to him to find out.

Dropping the ax, he gingerly wiped his bleeding hands across the front of his pants. He slipped to the side of the cabin and hid in its shadow. Poking his head around the corner, he was amazed at what he saw. He pulled his head back. Was his imagination running wild? Slowly he peeked around the corner again.

There, right in front of the cabin door, stood the biggest horse Charlie had ever seen. Its huge sides heaved and it seemed to snort steam into the wintry air. Its large feet stomped the ground and it tossed its monstrous, golden head and mane up and down and side to side. But, as magnificent as the horse was, what really demanded the boy's attention was the man sitting on top of the horse. For surely this was the biggest man he'd ever seen, a real giant of a man. His buckskin jacket was adorned with red, yellow, black, and white beads that were sprinkled across the broad chest and shoulders. Long, thin strips of leather dangled from the cuff of the sleeves all the way up to the underarm. His buckskin pants were tucked deep into dark leather moccasins that covered his legs from the knees down. A coonskin cap blended with his grayish-black hair and bushy beard. Charlie stood and stared, mouth agape and eyes wide, completely mesmerized by the sight of the mountain man and his horse.

11

"HELLO IN THE HOUSE," BOOMED THE big man.

Charlie jumped, startled by the cannon-like voice. He knew this was the customary greeting used by visitors when they approached isolated farmhouses. But he'd never seen or heard any visitor like this one. *What do I do?* he thought, leaning out of sight. The horse snorted and pawed at the ground as if anxious to move on. Not sure if he wanted them to stay, but afraid that they'd leave, Charlie cautiously emerged from his hiding place and approached the giants. Squinting into the afternoon sun that had just broken through the clouds, he sized up the visitors and figured them to be friendly.

"There's no need to yell, mister," said Charlie. "I'm the only one that'll be answerin' you, and I ain't deaf."

The big man turned to him and smiled a smile that animated his tanned face and made his gray eyes sparkle. "Sorry, son," said the stranger, his voice even and friendly.

"Guess I usually have to beller and it's become habit. Would it meet your approval if I lit off this animal for a spell?"

Staring up with one eye closed against the bright sun, the boy nodded. "I reckon it's okay."

The man swung a leg over and slid off the horse in one smooth motion, his feet never touching the stirrups. *Yep*, thought Charlie, *this here is the biggest man I've ever seen.* It seemed to him that the man stood about as tall as that she-grizzly and was just as broad.

The big man yawned and stretched his limbs. "Seems I been in this saddle for months. Feels good to get off and stand a while," he said.

Charlie shrugged his shoulders. "You're welcome to stand or sit, mister."

"Thanks." The stranger nodded. "Hey, you did a pretty good job of sneakin' up on me a minute ago. You know how to track and read sign?"

Charlie nodded. "I was taught by a Cherokee."

"Really? Well, I'll be." The stranger rubbed his whiskers and looked off into the distance, mumbling something about Cherokee being in these parts. Then he said, "Mind if I walk around?"

Still squinting, Charlie shook his head. "I don't mind, but there's not much to see, 'cept empty prairie in the front and big ol' trees in the back. There's a well over there," he added, pointing to one side, "if'n you'd like a drink."

"That sounds mighty refreshin', son," the man answered. "My horse and I been eatin' prairie dust for quite a while now. In fact," the big man tilted his head at the boy, "if *I'm* readin' sign right, looks like you've done worked up a sweat yourself. How 'bout joinin' me?"

"Yeah, I guess so."

The stranger held the reins of his horse and followed Charlie to the well. The boy tried not to limp and give away his injury. The horse found the trough without any problem. The stranger leaned against the aging stones as Charlie lowered the bucket into the dark well's water, gritting his teeth and holding his breath as he grasped the rope, not wanting to bring attention to his festered hands. But the big man had already taken note of the raw hands and the large red stain on Charlie's pant leg. Evidently not wanting to embarrass Charlie by mentioning it, though, he walked over and picked up the ax. "Looks like you've been tryin' your hand with this ax, boy. How'd you do?"

Charlie ladled some icy water from the bucket. "Not too good, mister," he answered. "Think I need a smaller ax. That one's too heavy for me. Can't get a good swing and I end up hittin' the ground more times than I hit the log."

With a couple of giant strides the man was back beside him. Accepting the ladle from Charlie, he drank long and slow. When he finished, he wiped his beard with the back of his sleeve and smiled down at the boy. "Water from a well," he said as he smacked his lips. "Nothin' quite like it. I'll have to tell you a story about that sometime." Pointing to the stump, he continued, "Anyway, it looks like you gave it a good run over there. I admire your determination. Mind if I try my hand at it now?"

Charlie took the ladle. "I don't mind," he said.

"Like to stretch my muscles after a long ride," replied the stranger.

"Oh." Charlie didn't understand why the man would want to chop wood after evidently traveling such a long distance, when he had the chance to sit and relax, but maybe he really did just want to stretch. Charlie certainly wasn't going to argue. He needed the help.

After the big man drank his fill of water, they approached the stump. The horse followed until he noticed a few still-green remnants of grass. The large animal, nibbling on his new-found feast, soon lost interest in what his master and the boy were doing with the big stick.

Hanging his hat on a pine branch, the stranger picked up the ax and swung it high over his head with the greatest of ease. *Well*, thought Charlie, *he must've traveled and stretched a lot in his day.* The ax came down straight and hard, splitting the log into two even pieces, sinking the blade deep into the stump. *He's got wood choppin' down pat, that's for sure.*

"Thanks for the water and the chance to stretch a bit," the man said. Then he split a few more logs. Charlie cleared his throat. "You're welcome mister. By the way, what's your name?"

The man looked surprised. "Well, I'll be," he said. He set the ax down and leaned on the handle, then pulled a colorful hanky from his back pocket and wiped the sweat from his face. "I done forgot the manners my mama made sure I learned. I'm sorry, son. Do you want my full name or the short version?"

Charlie smiled. "Well, let's start with the full name."

"Okay, the full name it is," replied the man. "But you've got to bear in mind that my ma was a God-fearin' woman and loved the Good Book, so she determined to name me after as many Bible men as she could." He chuckled. "If my pa hadn't stepped in, she prob'ly would've named me after all of 'em."

Charlie smiled at the thought.

The mountain man rubbed his chin as if trying to remember. "Now let's see, my full name is Jethro ... Ezekiel ... Samson ... " Charlie's eyes grew wider with every name. The stranger paused and stole a glance at the boy, then chuckled. "Aw, just call me Jess."

"Jess," said Charlie, squinting upward and smiling. "I like that name, and it'll be lots easier to remember."

"It will be that," Jess said. Motioning towards the horse, he continued, "And this here is my old friend, Goliath. I don't reckon he has a short version of his name, though." The horse lifted his head and regarded them for a second, but soon turned his attention to another clump of grass.

"He's *some* horse!" said Charlie.

"Yep, he's what they call a Belgian," explained Jess. "He's good for pullin' wagons and pushin' me around."

Charlie caught himself smiling again.

"He's broad in the backside, so a man has to have long enough legs to straddle him, but Goliath's a good horse, and I wouldn't trade him for any other." The horse lifted his head again and nickered at Jess as if to say, "Thanks, pardner. I wouldn't trade you, either."

"Well, Jess," said Charlie, "my full name is Charles Edward Smith, but ev'rybody calls me Charlie. I guess that's the short version of my name." Laughing, the big man and small boy went to shake hands, but then Jess hesitated and pulled his hand back, studying his palm.

"Excuse me, Charlie. It seems I got a mesquite thorn in my hand a while back and it'd be too sore to grab right now. Mind if we shake later, once it heals some?"

Not realizing the man was sparing *him* the pain, the boy nodded, "Sure, Jess. I understand."

Charlie returned to the well and ladled up more water while Jess went back to work on the woodpile. The boy watched as Jess cut about a week's worth of firewood before stopping to rest. Leaning on the ax handle again, he gulped down the water Charlie offered, then took out his hanky and mopped his face again. "Son, pardon me if I seem a bit nosey, but why is it that you're out here all by yourself?"

"I ain't really," mumbled the boy. "My Gramps is in the cabin, but he's sick. He's breathin' an' all, kinda raspy like, but he fell asleep one day and he hasn't woke back up. I don't know what's ailin' 'im. I feed 'im soup and water and try to keep 'im warm, but he just lays there sleepin'."

Resting the ax against the stump, Jess wiped his hands and arranged a few pieces of the deadwood into a seat. Sitting down, he motioned for the boy to sit as well. "How long's he been laid up, Charlie?" he asked gently.

The boy sat down on a log. He shook his head slowly. "I don't rightly know, Jess. Prob'ly a week or so, but it feels like a hundert years."

It was Jess's turn to look wide-eyed. "You mean to tell me you've been fetchin' for the two of you for a week or so, way out here alone?"

"Yessir. And I done okay till today when I tried choppin' wood. I knew that one was gonna be a problem."

"What about food, boy?"

"Oh, I can hunt some. Kilt us a rabbit and some squirrels not too long ago. I been stretchin' that pot of meat out for some time now."

"I see," nodded the man. "Had to cinch your belt up a notch or two, huh?"

Charlie stood and pulled up his baggy pants and tightened the leather strap. "Oh, that's nothin'. It's just an old belt. I've had plenty to eat."

"Ahh. Uh huh," nodded Jess as he leaned forward and rested his elbows on his knees, intertwining his fingers. "And how'd you get the bad leg?"

Charlie looked surprised. "Whatta you mean?"

"There's fresh blood on your pant leg, son. How bad are you hurt?"

Charlie twisted round and looked at the stain on his pants. He'd forgotten about it. Hesitant to answer, he cast his gaze to the ground. "It's not bad," he finally whispered.

"Charlie," Jess said, low and insistent. "How bad are you hurt?"

The boy's bottom lip quivered as he started to speak, so he bit it again. He turned and concentrated hard on the hills, but without permission a stream of tears started flowing down his cheeks.

"Bad enough, huh?" said Jess.

Charlie nodded.

"And more be hurtin' than just the hands and leg, I reckon."

Charlie just stared at him, offering no reply. Jess knelt on one knee and placed his big hands on the little shoulders. His gray eyes looked steadily into the brown eyes that tried to hide so much. "The heart's a funny thing, son," he said. "One minute it tells you to do somethin', and the next it scolds you for listenin', then it breaks because of it. You're more a man than most I've met. You did good, young man. Real good."

Charlie searched the eyes of the stranger. It felt as if he'd known him all his life. Who was he? The question rolled up from his soul, but stopped on his lips.

"Now, if'n it'd be okay, I'd like to take a look at your grandpa. And after that, I need to look at your injuries too," Jess said.

Charlie nodded again, still fighting tears. He didn't know this man, but somehow he knew he could trust him. There was just something about him. Without saying a word, Charlie motioned to the cabin and led him towards the back door. Jess got up and grabbed his cap, tucking it into the back of his britches as he followed the boy.

It took a while for their eyes to adjust to the darkness inside the cabin, with the only light coming from the small fire, but quickly things came into focus.

Jess looked around briefly. Directly opposite the back door was the front door. To his left was the kitchen area.

A couple of small shelves and a wooden cupboard hung on each side of a large, stone fireplace. A wooden plank that served as a counter for preparing meals was on one side of the fireplace and a smaller plank holding a wash basin was on the other. A square table and three chairs sat in the center of the room. To the right was a sitting area furnished with a small round table with an oil lamp, and beside it, a rocking chair. Several books were piled on the floor within reach of the chair. A worn, Indian rug covered the wood floor, lending the room a comfortable feeling. On the far wall, one small window provided the room's only source of natural light. Just beyond the sitting area, there was another door through which Charlie quietly led Jess, who had to duck as he followed Charlie into the room.

This room was quite small. It could only accommodate a double bed, a chest of drawers, a chair, and a bedside table, which held another oil lamp and a small, worn Bible. Jess noticed the book and smiled. There was one tiny window, so small that it limited the amount of sunlight allowed in the room.

On the bed lay the earthly vessel of a weathered old man. His frame was so thin, the bed covers barely outlined the body that lay beneath them. His stubbled face was pale and drawn, with ashen circles around his eyes and lips. His hands, lying loosely across his abdomen, looked almost translucent, revealing the blue veins that begrudgingly carried blood through his motionless body. His gray hair had lost its sheen and lay in tangled strands around his head and face. The room smelled of approaching death.

Charlie lit the oil lamp then waited in the doorway while Jess stood over Gramps, looking at him long and hard as if studying something Charlie couldn't see. He finally bent down and placed an ear on the old man's chest, listening. Then he raised up and laid a hand on Gramps' forehead for a few seconds. He gently stroked his cheek with a large, calloused hand and pushed strands of hair off his face. Then, without taking his eyes from the old man, Jess said, "Charlie, did you say your grandpa had a fever when he fell asleep?"

"I'm thinkin' he did, Jess, but not for long. Seems like it was just for the first couple of nights. I rubbed 'is head and arms with cool water like Grandma use to do for me when I was feelin' poorly. I never knew what good it did, but it always made me feel better, so I thought I'd try to make Gramps feel better too."

Glancing sideways at the boy, Jess nodded. "Good thinkin', son. You prob'ly saved his hide by doin' that. Does he take in much soup when you feed him?"

"A little bit," replied Charlie. "I only give 'im broth, 'cause I don't want 'im chokin' on meat. I keep givin' 'im sips till he doesn't swallow anymore."

Jess smiled. "Good job. You just keep on doin' what your doin' and Gramps'll be fine. He got a touch of pneumonia. His lungs are full, but they don't sound too bad. The sickness has weakened his heart, but he's come through the worst of it now."

Charlie limped over to Gramps and took a feeble hand in his. "Will he be wakin' up soon, Jess? I hope so."

Laying a hand on the boy's shoulder, Jess answered, "I can't tell when he'll come around exactly, but I reckon it'll be soon. How 'bout feedin' him some more of that broth."

Charlie sighed heavily. He stared at his grandpa for a moment longer, then turned and left the room.

"Got any extra night clothes for your grandpa?" Jess called from the bedroom.

Charlie turned from the cupboard. "Why?" he asked.

Jess's head poked around the corner. "'Cause we can't have him wakin' up in the same duds he's been wearin' for a few weeks, can we? Thought I'd clean him up a bit. Change the bed linens, too."

Charlie put the cup down and walked back into the room, the puzzled expression on his face.

"It'll be all right, boy, I promise. I just want to tidy Gramps up a bit. He's been fightin' hard to stay alive, but I figure when he does wake up, he'd appreciate not smellin' like he's died and come back."

Charlie stared up at the giant man. His frown gave way to a smile that slowly formed across his face as he thought about what Jess said. He pointed to the chest of drawers, "Nightshirt's in the second drawer. Linens are in the bottom."

"Good. Now you go finish fixin' his supper."

Charlie hesitated, then said, "Thank you, Jess. I, I couldn't—"

"It's okay, boy," assured the mountain man. "Everything's gonna be all right."

Charlie smiled again and headed back to the fireplace.

12

GRAMPS WAS WASHED UP AND TUCKED into clean blankets. Jess smiled down at the feeble old man. "My friend," he whispered, "you look better already."

Jess bowed his head. "Father, thank you for sparin' this child," he prayed. "It's your will that I'm here, so allow a good work to be done in him. Let your holy name be manifested and glorified through me. Amen."

In the other room, Charlie swung the iron kettle out from the warm fireplace and went through the routine of fixing his grandpa's supper. He served up a large portion of the stew for Jess and set it on the table along with some hard biscuits and a little jam. As Jess was ducking through the bedroom door, he met Charlie coming in to feed Gramps. "I fixed some for you too, Jess." Charlie motioned toward the table. "I'll join you in a bit."

Jess nodded. Knowing that the boy needed some time alone with his grandpa, Jess tossed the dirty linens into the basket under the counter and carried it outside to the large iron cauldron by the barn, which he filled with water. Then he lit a fire beneath it and waited for the flames to burn hot and steady. When the water started to steam, he took some time to snoop around in the barn. When his curiosity was satisfied, he went back into the cabin.

He added a couple of logs and stoked the fire. Then he opened the cupboards to take inventory of the small family's supplies. One cupboard had already been stocked with row after row of glass jars filled with home grown vegetables and fruit. In the next cupboard, Jess found that the shelves were short on dry goods like flour, sugar, salt, and coffee. "Looks like they could use some lard, bacon, raisins, and soap too," Jess muttered. Rummaging through the bags and boxes and tins, he completed his list, then turned to the stew and biscuits that Charlie had fixed for him, made himself comfortable, and dug in. About that time, Charlie came out of the bedroom, empty cup in hand. He'd finished the laborious job of getting the broth down Gramps.

The boy fixed a bowl of stew for himself and joined Jess. The rejuvenated fire had started to fill the room with its warmth, warding off the thin, unseen fingers of the cold evening air.

Jess chomped on a biscuit. "How old are you, son?"

"Ten," said Charlie. "But almost eleven," he quickly added. "My birthday's on Christmas."

"Well, I'll be," said Jess. "That'd be my birthday too."

Charlie glanced up at the mountain man. The boy looked surprised and a little comical with crumbs stuck to his bottom lip.

"Yep," confirmed the mountain man, "I was born on that very same day."

"Really?" asked the wide-eyed boy. "You and me have the same birthdays?"

Jess nodded. "Looks that way, son, although I ain't gonna be anywhere close to eleven." He laughed heartily. "Matter of fact, I can't recall how old I am, but I'd just as soon not know. Wouldn't do any good, just slow me down, I 'magine."

"Jess," asked Charlie, "where're you from?"

Jess stopped chewing and thought on the question. "Well, let's see," he started. "I was born somewhere out east, but I always tell folks I'm from the north, 'cause in reality, I've always been a mountain man. Folks relate mountains with the north, so that works."

Charlie looked confused. Jess laughed. "Let's just say I'm from way up yonder," pointing to the mountains behind the cabin. "Where're you from, Charlie?"

The boy swallowed. Using his sleeve, he wiped the biscuit crumbs from his face. "I was born in St. Louie, just like ev'ryone else in my family, but I came out here to live with Grandma and Gramps when my pa died."

Jess nodded. "So you see, you were born in one place, but come from another, just like me."

"Oh." Charlie smiled and added, "I see what you mean. I was born in St. Louie, but I'm from the Colorado Territory."

"Yep," replied Jess, "you got it."

When the two had finished their meal, Charlie tried to

stand up, but caught himself as pain shot up his leg. Jess jumped to his feet and commanded, "Stay where you are, son. Hand the cups to me and I'll take care of 'em after I look at your leg."

Charlie grew flustered. "I'm okay, Jess, really I am."

"Good," said Jess, "then there won't be too much fussin', but I still need to take a look."

The boy handed the cups to Jess then rolled the stiff, stained pant leg up over his calf. Jess reached down and offered him a hand, helping the boy to his feet. "Can you prop your leg up on the chair so I can study it closer?"

"I reckon." Charlie brought his knee up and rested his shin on the seat of the wooden chair.

"Hmmm," Jess muttered as he leaned over and looked at the wounds. He rubbed his chin. "Hmmm."

"'Tisn't that bad, Jess."

"Son, those are grizzly marks and you could've been killed. Looks like God was sure lookin' out for you."

"God wasn't nowhere around!" snapped the boy. "Hasn't been since Gramps got sick."

Jess paused and considered what Charlie said. He seemed ready to respond, but thought otherwise. Finally, he said, "Stay where you are, boy. You ripped a couple gashes open and they need cleanin' again."

Charlie glanced nervously back over his shoulder, "Are you gonna pour whiskey on it?"

"Naw," replied the man. "Good ol' hot water ought to do for now. But where in the world did you run into a grizzly?" he asked as he wiped the dried blood.

"Well," started Charlie, "It was a couple of days ago. I figured it was time I got us some more meat. You can only stretch rabbit so far, and after a while, you get tired of it."

Jess nodded, "Uh huh. Go on."

"So, I packed up my huntin' pouch—after tendin' to my chores here—then headed up the hills out back. I didn't go far, but had to climb up a ways before I seen deer tracks. Follered 'em for a while, but never saw nothin', so I decided to rest an' eat somethin'. It was then that I ran into the two bear cubs, playin' nice an' all. They didn't pay no mind to me, and I didn't do nothin' to them."

Jess dabbed at the wounds carefully. "But mama was standin' close by and didn't take all your good intentions into consideration, now did she?" he asked.

Charlie began to feel uneasy. The memory was too fresh. Tension filled his voice. "Nope, she didn't. She reared up, roared till I was pretty near deaf, then before I knew it ..." Charlie swallowed, then continued, "She charged me. Lucky for me, there was a clump of trees nearby, so I hid in there till she left to go after somethin' else." He cast a quick glance down at his leg, then whispered, "She got me before I was all the way in, though."

Beads of sweat had formed across his forehead. "Didn't think I was gonna make it," he added, barely audibly.

After a quiet moment, Jess asked, "Why did you take the big gun?"

The question caught Charlie by surprise. How'd he know there was a big gun?

"My gun can't kill no deer," he whined defensively.

Jess stayed calm. "So, your grandpa didn't mind you usin' his gun, alone or otherwise?"

Charlie grew perplexed. "No," he nipped.

Jess glanced at the fireplace. "Where is it now?"

Charlie hesitated, not sure how to respond. Then he answered briskly, "I lost it."

Jess stopped cleaning the wound. "You lost it?" his voice rose in disbelief.

Charlie held his breath and stared straight ahead, afraid to turn and meet the disapproving eyes of the big mountain man. The moment felt like an eternity to the boy and soon his defenses began to fall and his anger turned to shame.

After a few seconds, Jess repeated the question, his voice softer, but still reflecting his disappointment. "So, it's gone?"

"Yeah," mumbled Charlie. "I'd give anything to get it back, but I'm not right sure where I dropped it, or I'd go fetch it." He could feel his cheeks burn as another lie poured from his lips. Charlie knew exactly where he'd dropped the gun, he just couldn't admit to himself or to Jess that he was too afraid to go get it.

Jess sighed and slapped the sides of his legs. "Well, we'll not worry 'bout that right now," he whispered. "I'm sure your grandpa will understand. After all, he can't get upset with you for losin' his gun if he's the one who gave you permission to go out by yourself and hunt with it and all, now can he?"

Charlie started to protest, but changed his mind. "Yeah," he stammered. "I guess."

"And if God wasn't around, we can't ask Him for help, 'cause He wouldn't have a clue what we're talkin' about," Jess added, stealing a glance over at the boy. Charlie grew quiet again.

Jess finished cleaning the wounds and helped Charlie with his pant leg. Then without a word, he stepped back outside to check on the laundry. Charlie gathered the cups and bowls and placed them in the water basin. His hands and leg hurt, but not as bad as his heart.

13

CHARLIE SAT AT THE TABLE AND BURIED his face in his arms. What he had said about God, about Gramps and the gun, it was wrong, all of it. He knew that. But he couldn't help how he felt. Heaven had sent no message of comfort, no direction, nothing for him to hold onto when it seemed his heart was pleading the most sincerely and desperately for God's help. How could he credit God with saving his life if all he got back from his prayers was silence?

His thoughts were interrupted by Jess's voice calling from outside. "Charlie, come on out here, son. I got the tub ready."

Charlie lifted his head. "Tub? Whatta you mean, *tub*?" Confused, he limped to the door and looked out.

Jess pointed to the barn. "I found an old bathtub in the barn and figured you could use it," he said with a grin.

"But it's freezin' out here," Charlie protested. "Me and Gramps take baths in the warmer months, but not in the wintertime. Can't I just boil another pot of water and clean up that way?"

"Nope," answered Jess. "Your wounds need cleanin' through and through and your muscles need soothin'. Nothin' better than a good hot bath to take care of both them needs. Besides, where you're gonna be sittin', it ain't freezin'." He laughed. "Now, grab some clean clothes and get out here."

Charlie looked back at the mountain man with growing frustration and rolled his eyes. But Jess held steadfast and smiled. "It's time to clean house, Charlie," he gently scolded. "All of it. Inside and out. We got Gramps taken care of, and now it's your turn."

Charlie sighed and shook his head, sensing it was useless to argue. He found a clean pair of long johns, socks, and a pair of jeans. Tucking those under his arm, he grabbed a towel from underneath the counter and stepped outside. The cold wind blew hard against him and he hobbled as fast as he could toward the barn.

"Don't know what difference it'll make," he grumbled. "Hot water is hot water. It's not been that long since I cleaned up." Stopping, he thought for a second. "Okay," he admitted, "It's been a while since I cleaned up in the tub, but I still don't know what difference it makes. It's just me an' Gramps here, anyway."

The old barn offered some shelter, but it wasn't as warm in there as in the cabin. *Just grit your teeth an' get this over with,* Charlie thought as goose bumps stood up on his arms. He found the tub sitting in an empty stall. Jess had thrown blankets over the half-walls to create some privacy. Fresh hay lay scattered on the floor, its aroma heightened by the bath's vapors. Charlie watched the steam spiral upward from the tub. "It does look kinda invitin'," he whispered. The boy stepped closer and dipped his hand into the hot liquid, swirling it with his fingers.

"Throw your clothes over the wall," called Jess. "Might as well wash them along with the other clothes an' things."

Shivering, Charlie got out of his clothes as fast as he could and threw them over to Jess. The wind whipped round the corners of the barn, rattling the walls and the tools that hung from their pegs. It rattled everything, right down to Charlie's teeth. There was no turning back now. He climbed into the hot water. Then, sinking into the deep tub, he found instant refuge from the cold.

The boy rested his head against the warm metal and closed his eyes, noticing for the first time how tight his neck muscles were; his shoulders were pulled up around his ears, and his nerves felt strained and taut. Slowly he relaxed his shoulders and stretched his limbs. The wounds on his hands and legs revolted against the heat at first, but eventually they too accepted its healing embrace. The sweet smell of the hay, mingled with the scent of the animals, comforted the boy, easing him deeper into the water, revitalizing his wounded body and spirit.

Outside, Jess stirred the bundle of soiled material down into the kettle and watched as the colorful mixtures of cloth sank beneath the boiling foam. He watched until three or four bubbles appeared at one time, then he went over to the stump and sat down, listening to the wind. "Snows a'comin'," he whispered. "Pretty soon, everything will be white as snow." Jess closed his eyes and drew a long, deep breath of the cold air. Exhaling slowly, he relaxed and appeared lost in thought.

"Jess," whispered Charlie, right beside the stump where Jess sat dreaming.

Charlie's voice startled the big man so much that his eyes popped open and he jumped and that in turn startled Charlie. In the moment of surprise and confusion, Jess lost his balance. Giant feet and arms flailed in the air as he desperately tried to keep from falling off the stump. His coonskin cap flew off. Charlie stumbled backwards, but righted himself by grabbing Jess's hand. The big man settled himself back up on his roost, and they both laughed until tears ran down their cheeks.

Catching his breath, Jess stood and ran his fingers through his thick, unruly hair, then realized he'd lost his hat. He bent to retrieve it and gave it a shake then placed it firmly on his head, with the coon tail going down the back. He grinned at Charlie. "I meant to do that, you know."

"Sure, I know." Charlie giggled. "You didn't see me, but you could hear me, right?"

"Spoken like a true tracker." Jess laughed, then looked directly into Charlie's eyes. "Are you feelin' better, now?" he asked.

"Yeah," Charlie had to admit. He felt warm inside in spite of the chilly air on the outside.

"Good. Now, go on in by the fire and rub your head dry while I finish with the linens. I'll be in shortly." The big mountain man grinned from ear to ear.

"Okay," Charlie said and then turned toward the cabin. Halfway there, he looked over his shoulder at the big man. "Thanks, Jess," he added. He felt good saying that.

The mountain man finished wringing and hanging the laundry then secured the animals for the night. Nellie and Bessie were tucked comfortably in their stalls and the chickens were nestled together in their coop. Goliath was too big for the barn, so Jess tied him to a clump of scrub oaks. Those would have to do for shelter tonight. He fed fresh oats to the horses and whispered to his regal animal that tomorrow he would start constructing him proper accommodations.

Inside, Charlie dried his hair with a towel to ward off the cold, still laughing about such a big man fighting so hard to keep from falling off a stump. Jess came in and finished cleaning the kitchen then sat on the floor near the warm fire. Grabbing a book, he flipped through the pages of a worn classic while Charlie hung the towel on a hook and combed his hair.

"Do you know how to read these books, Charlie?"

"I can read some," he replied. "Grandma was teachin' me before she died, then Gramps read to me almost ev'ry night. I remember some of the words."

"Want me to teach you some more?"

Charlie shrugged his shoulders. "Sure, don't see how it would hurt none."

The big man smiled and patted the floor beside him. "Good, then come on over here and let's get started with our first readin' lesson."

Charlie eased himself down beside the big man. Before long, the two were lost in the magical tale of a crotchety old miser and the soul-saving search for the true spirit of Christmas in a book entitled *A Christmas Carol*, by a man named Charles Dickens. As Jess helped Charlie sound out the words, the boy's imagination took him far beyond the hand-hewn walls of the little cabin and into the streets of Queen Victoria's London.

"Ma-rr-la," he said, stumbling over the word.

"Marley," Jess corrected.

Charlie looked up and smiled. Continuing on, he read, "Marley was dead, to begin with. There is no dubt whatever about that."

"Very good," said Jess. "That word is *doubt* though, not *dubt*. Try it again."

Charlie struggled with the words a while longer. Jess let him struggle, instructing him to sound out the consonants first, then the vowels, until he reached the proper conclusion. Reading the sentences again, Charlie began to grasp their full and intended meaning.

Submerged in the story, the boy wanted to read on, but his eyelids grew heavy. The warm bath had worked its magic on his aching body. He handed the book to Jess. "Will you read the story now, and I'll just listen for a while?"

"Sure, son," answered the mountain man. "Be glad to."

Holding the small book in his huge hands, Jess read with enthusiasm, painting on the canvass of Charlie's imagination, using the words of Mr. Dickens as the brush strokes that shaped each picture. Enthralled by the story, Charlie felt he was there in the secluded chamber of Scrooge's home, watching his internal struggle with destiny. He was unconvinced by Scrooge's argument that the translucent messenger was merely the result of undigested food. In his mind he stepped through the imaginary window that led Scrooge and Marley to the edge of the mysterious spiritual realm where Marley bewailed his weighted and eternal curse. But alas, even Jess's lively reading couldn't keep the tired boy awake for long. Setting the book aside, Jess looked at the small form that was curled up close to his side. He softly stroked the boy's cheek with his burly fingers and whispered, "Suffer the little children to come unto me."

Tenderly gathering the boy in his arms, Jess knelt where he was and bowed his head. "Thank you, Father, for this child so brave," he prayed. "Heal his wounds, on the inside as well as the outside, and give him a peaceful night's sleep."

Jess tucked Charlie into his bedroll and waited until he was sound asleep. Then, grabbing his jacket and cap, he walked out into the darkness to check on Goliath.

In the bedroom Gramps' eyelids fluttered.

14

CHARLIE AWOKE TO THE AROMA OF FRESH-
baked biscuits. He rubbed the sleep from his eyes and
waited for the remains of a wonderful dream to dissipate
and his dreadful existence to come back into focus. It must
have been a dream. Mountain men don't just show up
during a storm in December and do all your work for you,
and help you forget your fears, and even make you laugh.

But to Charlie's great relief, although the big man was
nowhere to be seen at the moment, Jess's bedroll was folded
neatly in the corner, proving that yesterday was a day in his
real past, not one in his imagination.

Slowly getting to his feet, Charlie noted that the struggle to stand up wasn't as rough as it had been; his leg
felt better than it had the day before. He folded his blankets, laid them next to Jess's, and went to the table. Sure
enough, nestled in a napkin-covered basket were twelve
puffy, golden biscuits. A small bowl of jam and a plate of
butter had been placed beside them. His mouth watered

and his jaw muscles contracted in anticipation. He could hardly wait to dig in but thought twice about it and went to find Jess first.

He swung the front door open to the bright sun and frigid wind. Well, winter had definitely come, and was unquestionably still here. Squinting, Charlie scanned the prairie. Just then, from behind the house, came the sound of cracking wood. Relieved, he grabbed his jacket from its peg and hurried round to the barnyard.

Jess looked up and smiled, but continued to work. "Good mornin', son," he said. "How'd you sleep?"

"Mornin', Jess. I slept fine. How 'bout you?"

"Like a log. I was plum tuckered, I guess." He swung the ax high above his head, then brought it down with tremendous force, instantly splitting the log in two. A sharp *crack!* bounced up the hills. "You eat them biscuits yet?"

Charlie pushed his hands inside his jacket pockets. He hadn't yet realized that the swelling had left them and they were free from the intense stinging that had plagued him for days. All he could think about was how promising this day looked.

"No, sir, but they sure look an' smell mighty good. Have you ate some yet?"

Jess stacked the split timber onto the woodpile. "Yep, I sure did," he said. "Et about twelve of them things before sunup. Went ahead and made another batch just for you." Picking up the ax, he laughed heartily.

Charlie smiled and again he felt warm inside. But his stomach was growling.

Jess nodded towards the cabin then swung the ax over his head again. "Go back in the house and eat your fill, 'cause after that we got work to do."

Charlie nodded and gladly headed back inside, as another *whack!* thundered up through the trees.

The biscuits were still warm and the butter melted as fast as Charlie could spread it. He dolloped berry jam and ate the first biscuit in two bites. Then he ate one after another, rinsing down each one with gulps of cold milk. It was the best breakfast he'd had in a long time. When he finished, he cleaned the kitchen and fixed a cup of broth for Gramps and took it into the bedroom for his morning visit.

Gramps was lying still and peaceful, just as he expected, but the old man's color had changed a little. The ashen lips revealed a hint of fleshy pink, as did his cheeks and hands, but this didn't excite the boy too much, considering that Gramps still hadn't moved or opened his eyes.

"Got us a visitor, Gramps." Charlie talked quietly as he fed the old man. "His name is Jess. You'd like 'im."

Charlie concentrated on getting another spoonful into his grandpa's mouth without making too much of a mess. "He's been a big help 'round here. 'Specially with the firewood. Came right in the nick of time, he did."

The old man's breathing quickened slightly. Afraid his grandpa was about to choke, Charlie stopped talking until the breathing returned to normal. "Okay, finish your breakfast, and I'll tell you more when you get better."

Charlie took care of the inside chores, then grabbed

his jacket again and headed outside to help Jess. The wind came across the prairie, and he stopped and listened for the familiar rush through the trees and the moan of the branches as the gust crashed like breakers against the hills. The sound didn't bother him so much now.

Charlie tended to the animals and then watched Jess finish chopping a branch down to size and begin to neatly stack the pieces in what was shaping up to be a nice-sized woodpile. Stopping to wipe his brow, Jess took the liberty of showing Charlie how he could help. They worked steadily; only breaking a couple of times to feed Gramps and to grab some fast sandwiches of leftover biscuits and jerky.

By the end of the day, the woodpile had grown considerably; Charlie had gathered a significant amount of prairie grass which would be used as bedding to keep Goliath, Nellie, and Bessie warm and fed during the winter; the roof of the cabin had been reinforced; and the barn for Goliath was near completion. It wasn't really a barn, more like a lean-to, a three-sided shelter to keep the huge horse dry when it snowed and to protect him from the wind.

After supper Jess and Charlie settled down for another reading lesson, but before they could finish half a page, the boy had again fallen asleep on the big man's arm. Jess gently laid the sleeping boy on his bedroll and tucked him in.

With Charlie asleep, Jess sat against the wall and looked through the books on the floor. Remembering the Bible in Gramps' room, he tiptoed in to fetch it off the bedside table. As he reached down for it, he glanced at the old man and caught a slight movement of his eyelids.

"Well now," Jess whispered. "Are you finally wakin' up, my friend? I know one boy who'll be happier than a bear in salmon season." He chuckled softly. "Tell you what. I was just gettin' ready to read from the Good Book, so why don't I just read to you. How's that sound?"

Not waiting for a response, Jess sat at the foot of the bed and started reading. First, the two ventured across the Sinai desert with the Israelites, discussing in mono-logue the stubbornness of mankind. Moving into the New Testament, he read the familiar story of the virgin birth, marveling at the wonders of Heaven's plan. Although the conversation was one-sided, Jess seemed to thoroughly enjoy the Bible study and he thanked Gramps for sharing the time with him.

"Would you like me to pray for you, Stuart?" he whis-pered. Gramps' eyelids fluttered and Jess smiled as he bowed his head. Quietly, he stood before the throne and in fervent whispers sought God's comfort for the boy who lay in the next room, struggling with secrets that tormented his soul, and then for God's healing of the old man who lay here wanting to go home, but his mission incomplete. And then for himself, that he would be ready and willing to do all that was asked of him, no matter how hard the task. Then he opened his eyes and smiled at Gramps. "Not yet, Stuart," he whispered. "Not yet."

15

JESS CUT ENOUGH FIREWOOD DURING the next several days to get Charlie and his grandpa through the winter. Goliath's lean-to was finished, and enough game had been killed and cleaned to feed them for quite a few weeks. Charlie dug the last of the potatoes and carrots from the garden and gathered prairie grass. It kept the boy busy enough not to worry about his grandpa during the day and tuckered out enough to sleep like a baby at night. But lately it wasn't only Gramps that worried Charlie. He had another question on his mind.

One night, after a long day of chores, Jess prepared a hearty supper of venison steak and vegetables, which Charlie lauded as his favorite meal. Jess proved to be a good cook, but then anything was better than what Charlie himself could fix, and that just about summed up the problem.

Maybe you better learn how to cook like this while you can, Charlie told himself. *Jess's not gonna be here forever.* The thought had been gnawing at him for days. What if Jess did leave? No one said he had to stay. Things around the farm were pretty much under control. Why, Jess could pick up and head out anytime he wanted to.

Charlie squirmed at the thought of being alone again. He barely swallowed his bite of carrot before blurting out the question, "Our birthdays are just a few days off, Jess. Are you gonna be here for our birthdays?"

Jess laid his fork and knife on his plate and gazed steadily into the boy's eyes. "Well, son, I've been givin' that some thought and with your permission, I think there are a few more things I need to tend to. So, yes, I'd like to be here for our birthdays."

Charlie nodded and slid another bite of cooked carrots into his mouth, trying not to reveal his insecurity and relief.

Then Jess spoke again. "How far is it to town, son?"

The boy's eyes widened and a frown furrowed his brow. "'Bout a day's ride to the south," he stated, then quickly added, "Why? You aren't goin', are you?"

"Yep," replied Jess. "You and your grandpa need some vittles stored up before winter sets in. And while I'm in town, I think I'll hop into the stores and see what other things they might have of interest, too. Is there anything you might be hankerin' for, or anything that Gramps might need once he wakes up?"

Turning a potato over and over with his fork, Charlie quietly answered, "No. I never give it much thought, but I don't think so."

"Well, with your birthday comin' up an' all, is there anything you'd like to have? I mean, a boy only turns eleven once," said Jess, smiling.

"No," whispered Charlie. "There's nothin' I really want or need 'cept my Gramps, so, unless you can bring *him* back to me, you don't need to worry 'bout gettin' me anythin' else."

Jess finished chewing a bite. "Well then, I reckon I'll just go get them vittles."

With his heart thumping in his ears, Charlie didn't hear those last three words. He only heard that Jess planned to leave. Apprehension began to overpower his rational thought and the terror of being alone again seized him. He was going to wake up from this dream after all. He was about to come face to face with his worst fear again. Jess was going to leave. His head started to swim. To have to make decisions alone, decisions that he wasn't ready to make meant having to deal with the failures that come from making the wrong decisions, which he always seemed to do. He couldn't bear the thought of his failures mocking him for his weak attempts at being a man. He sat motionless for a few minutes, staring at the floor. Then without a word he pushed his plate away and went to the fireplace to fix Gramps a cup of broth.

Jess stopped eating and slowly laid his fork aside. "You okay, Charlie?" he asked.

The boy stopped what he was doing and grabbed the edge of the counter to support himself as he tried to regain control, but his heart wouldn't listen to his brain. Feelings overwhelmed him. His shoulders slumped and his chin fell to his chest. Breathing heavily, he choked back tears, and out tumbled the words, "Are you comin' back, Jess?" He turned to the big man. Tears streamed down his face. "You'll come back, won't you?"

Jess stood up and stepped back from the table. With that step, Charlie's heart broke. He ran to the big man and threw his arms around his waist, his silent tears turning into tumultuous sobs. Jess fell to his knees and let the boy bury his face in his large shoulder. In between sobs, Charlie tried to tell Jess what it was like being alone with no one to care or help. He tried to tell him how he worked hard and wanted to do the right things, only to find himself in pain for his efforts. He tried to tell how scared he was: scared of the wind, scared of the outside, scared of everything. But all that came out of his mouth were garbled words, muffled by sobs that shook his entire frame. Jess closed his eyes and listened. He understood everything.

"Don't leave me, Jess," begged Charlie. "Please don't leave me."

Holding the boy in his arms, Jess kissed the top of his head and whispered, "Now there, son, don't be afraid. I ain't gonna leave you. I promise, Charlie, I won't ever leave you." The little boy, frozen with fear, began to soften as the man's soothing voice calmed his raging inner storm.

"I'm just goin' to town to get some vittles and such, Charlie. I'll only be gone for three days. Two days ridin' and one day providin'. That's all, just three days." Jess held the boy for as long as he needed to be held, letting him cry until he was all cried out.

His sobs eventually melted. Jess gave him a gentle squeeze and wiped the tears from the freckled face. "No need to worry, Charlie," he said with a smile. "You an' Gramps are in the best of hands. I'll leave at first light and come back on the third day. You got my word on that."

Charlie sniffled and wiped his face with the back of his sleeve. "Promise?" he asked.

Smoothing Charlie's brown hair with his fingers, Jess grinned. "I promise, little man."

16

SHADOWS AND FIRELIGHT DANCED ACROSS the ceiling as Jess and Charlie lay in their bedrolls, hands tucked under their heads, listening to the wind blow across the prairie and up through the trees.

"Jess?" Charlie whispered.

"Yes, son."

"What'd you mean earlier when you said that me an' Gramps was in the best of hands?"

"I meant that you an' your grandpa are in the Father's hands, Charlie. He'll watch over you while I'm gone."

Charlie didn't respond.

"Charlie?"

"Yep, Jess."

"You believe that, don't you?"

Charlie sighed with uncertainty. "I guess you mean God." He thought a moment, then continued, "It was easy to believe in God before Gramps got sick. He and Grandma taught me from the Bible and prayed with me ev'ry night. But it seemed like after Grandma died and then Gramps got sick, God went away."

"God went away?" asked Jess.

Charlie sighed again. "It sure seemed like it. I don't know how many times I asked Him to help Gramps, to bring 'im back, but he's still a' lyin' back there, sick as ever. No matter what I tried to do, he just wouldn't get better, and God doesn't seem to hear me, or maybe He just doesn't care."

Jess rolled onto his side and leaned on his elbow to face the boy. "Well, have you ever thought that if you hadn't been prayin' for Gramps, he might've up and died a long time ago? … That maybe you askin' God for help actually kept your grandpa alive longer than he otherwise might've been?"

Charlie blinked and stared harder at the ceiling. "I never thought 'bout it like that."

"Sometimes," Jess continued, "the Father works a little slower than we'd like Him to, 'cause He doesn't live by the same clock we do, but He always has a plan, Charlie. Maybe He wants somethin' more than just your grandpa gettin' better, son. Maybe God wants Charlie, too."

Confused, Charlie turned and looked at Jess questioningly.

Jess maintained his course. "Like I said, Charlie, the Father always has a plan. Gramps gettin' sick, you needin' help, me comin' along. All that wasn't by chance; it was part of His plan. But before God shows us the outcome, He wants to make sure that everyone understands who gets the applause. See Charlie, God wants all the glory. He doesn't want confusion about who did what. He wants everyone to know that it was Him, that we owe the thanksgivin' to Him."

"But if God brought Gramps back when I asked 'im to, I woulda known it was *Him* who did it."

"Really?" asked Jess. "How would you 'ave known that?"

"'Cause I asked 'im to do it."

"Yeah," Jess agreed. "But maybe if Gramps got better right away, you would've thought it was because of what you did for your grandpa, like feedin' him broth an' wipin' him down with cool water to stop the fever. Remember Charlie, God doesn't work on our clock, and He'll wait as long as it takes till we reach that point when we will know for sure that the answer came from Him and no one else."

"Shouldn't I ha' given Gramps the broth and the water?" asked Charlie.

Jess chuckled affectionately. "You did the right things, son. You took care of your grandpa and kept him alive by doin' what you did. God uses people to do what He wants done, but if Gramps continues to live, if he gets better, it will be 'cause the Father chooses life for him."

Charlie lay quietly and listened as Jess told him about Jesus, the only begotten Son of the Father, and how God loved the world so much that Jesus willingly died on the cross so each and every person could go to Heaven.

"You know the Christmas story, don't you, Charlie?"

"Sure, Jess."

"And you know the Easter story, about when Jesus was crucified, but rose from the dead on the third day?"

"Yep, Grandma taught me that, too."

"Bless Grandma's heart," whispered the mountain man. "Well, do you know *why* Jesus was born here on earth and then died on the cross?"

"Grandma said it was to take away our sin."

"And she was exactly right. He died so that He could save anyone who asked for forgiveness of their sin. Have you ever done that, Charlie?"

"Done what?"

"Asked Jesus to forgive you of your sin, come into your heart, and be your Savior?"

"I don't think so, Jess."

Charlie listened as Jess explained how Adam and Eve were "kicked out" of the garden and how after that they had to work hard to live. But the most hurtful punishment of all was the broken fellowship with God.

Charlie nodded in agreement. "Gramps an' me, we always had to work hard, but when we worked t'gether it wasn't so bad." His voice dropped to a whisper. "But now I know how it feels to be alone and tryin' to work hard to survive."

"Yeah. Adam and God used to walk in the garden together ev'ry evening. They made plans together and worked together to make the garden even more beautiful and fruitful." Jess grew silent a moment, then added, "But then Adam sinned by doing the one thing that God had told him not to do—"

Charlie glanced at the place where Big Blue had hung, now looking so empty and so accusing.

"—then Adam was alone in his work," continued Jess. "He didn't get to walk ev'ry day with God and have His constant help anymore."

"All because of just that one thing he did?"

"Yes, Charlie. 'That one thing he did' was that he disobeyed. And the fact is, disobedience is sin. And sin puts a separation between you an' God."

Charlie kept silent, thinking hard. Then he said, "Jess, do you think maybe Adam thought he could give *himself* permission to go ahead an' eat the fruit that God told 'im not to eat?"

"Yes I do, Charlie."

"Like maybe it seemed so right and God wasn't there walkin' with 'im right then, and Adam had to make a decision all on 'is own?"

"Every man has to choose on his own sometime, Charlie. And everyone who has ever lived has chosen to sin, just like Adam an' Eve did."

"When a fella chooses to sin, things can get pretty messed up, can't they?"

"Yes, son. Fact is, it leaves a big ol' empty place in your heart."

Charlie felt a heaviness in his chest, a secret that was weighing on him. *It's been so good to have Jess here an' have 'is help,* he thought, *but he can't help me get out of this fix. If I tell 'im ev'rything, he'll get mad an' leave.* As he lay there looking at that empty place above the mantel—empty and accusing, like the big empty place in his heart—the feelings of failure came rushing back. Charlie rolled over onto his side, his back to Jess. The burden of the secret of how he'd disobeyed the one thing Gramps said not to do, not to do ever, weighed heavier with every sigh.

What if Gramps got up right now and came in here? He'd see that 'is gun is gone, Charlie thought. *How would I explain what I did?* Since Jess had showed up, Charlie had been able to put all that failure out of his mind. After all, Jess didn't know the real reason why he lost Big Blue. But Gramps—Would Gramps be mad and not talk to him anymore? Could he forgive Charlie for what he'd done? He'd be disappointed for sure. Charlie closed his eyes in despair. *What am I gonna do?*

"Charlie," whispered Jess. The big man's voice softly summoned the boy, but Charlie didn't want to talk anymore. He ignored the call and closed his eyes. Jess lay back on his bedroll and prayed.

17

JESS WAS GONE WHEN CHARLIE AWOKE, but breakfast was still warm and waiting for him on the table. He ate, then took care of Gramps. After cleaning up the utensils, he grabbed his jacket from the peg and walked outside. The lean-to was empty. Not a sound could be heard except the rustling of dry leaves on the ground and wind in the trees. The loneliness felt worse than before.

He took his time milking Nellie and grooming Bessie, trying to keep busy as the morning hours slowly passed. The chickens were the only ones who got excited, flapping up toward the bucket of corn, impatient with his slowness in pouring it out for them. "Hey, hold your horses!" Charlie scolded them.

In the afternoon, he cut a little prairie grass, then he just leaned against the back of the cabin, looking up at the hills and thinking of Big Blue.

Somewhere up there lay Gramps' one true treasure. *I'll hafta find a way to go look for it.* The thought surprised him.

"Oh no, you won't," he scolded himself aloud. "You ain't doin' nothin' of the sort." Turning, he darted into the cabin, as if the closed door would erase the responsibility.

Inside, Charlie made himself comfortable on the chair beside his grandpa's bed and opened the book about Scrooge and his strange visitors, sounding out the words, reading as best he could. Glancing at Gramps in between sentences, he thought he saw a slight movement of his eyelids.

"What was that?" Charlie exclaimed. "Gramps, did you flutter your eyes at me? Can you hear me, Gramps?" He tossed the book onto the bedside table and leaned over the old man, watching his face intently.

"I know I saw you move, Gramps," he whispered. "I know I did. Can you hear me, Gramps?"

The old man's eyelids fluttered again.

"Yes! I knew it." Charlie was so excited, he could hardly breathe for a moment. Then he jumped, whooped and laughed as tears ran down his cheeks. After weeks of nothing, his grandpa had finally moved!

Charlie jumped onto the bed, landing on all fours, and planted a kiss on his grandpa's forehead. He sat back on his heels and searched the old man's face, waiting for his eyes to flutter again. Waiting in the stillness of the room, he realized that the pain in his leg was gone. Then he held up his hands and turned them over and over, searching for the remnant of a blister or a scar from a splinter, but there were none to be found.

"Well, lookit that. I'm all better too," he whispered.

The anticipation during the next couple of days was almost unbearable for the boy. Gramps was fluttering his eyes more now as if he wanted to open them, but didn't have the strength. Charlie ignored what chores he could, staying by his grandpa's side, leaving only when it was necessary.

The evening before Jess was to return, Charlie picked up Gramps' Bible, turning the worn pages with careful fingers. In some of the margins, Gramps had written notes of how the verses moved him, how the Lord spoke to him through its message. Tenderly, Charlie turned to the front leaf of the book, and there someone had written an inscription that was now almost too faint to read. It spoke of a true friendship and how the giver would never leave Gramps. It was signed, but the name was too faded to read except for the last two letters: "---*us.*"

"I wonder who gave you this Bible, Gramps," Charlie whispered. He tried to think of familiar names that ended with '-*us,*' but none came to mind. He couldn't think of anyone in the family, past or present, or any close friends whose names ended that way. Charlie sat the book back down. "I'll ask Gramps 'bout that when he wakes up."

On the third morning, just after sunrise, Charlie heard horse hooves beating across the hard ground. Jess was back! He threw the blankets aside, jumped up, grabbed his jacket, and ran outside. There was Goliath, galloping towards the cabin with Jess on his back, smiling and waving. Bags and packages of all shapes and sizes were strapped to Goliath's saddle and bounced to and fro with his heavy strides. The boy laughed at the sight.

As they got closer to the house, Charlie ran out to meet them. "Gramps's been fluttering 'is eyelids, Jess. He moved!"

Jess slowed Goliath to a trot, then reined him in at the door. "Well, how 'bout that?" he replied as he swung his leg—fringes flying—over the horse's back, and jumped to the ground, still holding the reins. "How long's he been doin' that, Charlie?"

"Ever since you left, Jess. I been readin' to 'im and I noticed 'is eyelids movin' a little bit," Charlie said excitedly. "Now he's gettin' real handy at it. I think he's tryin' to say somethin'." Charlie paused to catch his breath.

Jess patted him on the back. "I'd say he is, Charlie. He's tryin' to tell you to hang in there and keep believin'. He's on his way back."

Unloading the packages off Goliath's back, Jess handed Charlie two bags at a time to take into the cabin. The boy impatiently ran them into the kitchen and sat them wherever he could find a place, scattering bags throughout the room. It wasn't until Goliath was unsaddled, brushed down, and resting in his lean-to that Jess ducked into the bedroom to see Gramps. Charlie followed close behind. The old man was lying there still as ever, but Jess could see a difference. He pulled at his beard and kept repeating, "Hmmm."

"Looks like most of his color has come back, son," Jess announced after he'd studied Gramps' face. "His breathin' isn't so labored, either." Jess nodded with approval. "Yep, he looks mighty fine to me. Shouldn't be too long till Gramps is up an' movin' around, as fit as a fiddle."

Charlie was beaming. This must be the answer to his prayers.

"How 'bout some breakfast, son?" asked Jess. "I got bacon in one of them bags. I'll fry us some thick slices of bacon and make my favorite flapjacks if'n that'll be okay with you."

Smiling up at the big man and suddenly realizing that his stomach was growling, Charlie agreed. "That'd be fine, Jess."

≋ 18 ≋

TO CHARLIE'S DELIGHT, THEIR MORNING feast consisted of dark coffee, thick bacon, and buttermilk flapjacks dripping with sweet butter and warm maple syrup.

Charlie licked the syrup from the corners of his mouth. "Jess?" he asked.

"Yep, Charlie?"

"Would you mind if I stayed with Gramps today, instead of cuttin' prairie grass?"

Jess stopped chewing and looked directly at the boy, concern in his gray eyes, but Charlie had his mind on something and didn't notice.

"What're you plannin' on doin'?" Jess asked.

"Nothin' much, 'cept readin' to 'im," replied the boy. "I just wanna be with 'im in case he opens 'is eyes, that's all."

Jess hesitated, then nodded. He finished chewing his bite and swallowed. "I reckon so, if that's what you choose to do. But if you need anything, just holler. I'll be close by."

"Thanks, Jess." Charlie absentmindedly shoveled another forkful of flapjack into his mouth.

The two finished their meal and straightened up the kitchen. Jess strode outside into the crisp morning air, while Charlie went into the bedroom. Once the boy heard the sharp crack of the ax, he leaned closer to his grandpa's ear.

"I know you'll be wakin' up soon, Gramps," he whispered. "So before you do, I've gotta go find somethin'. I won't be gone long, I promise." He kissed the old man on the forehead and turned to leave, but thought of something else. "Oh, an' remember. You're not alone, Gramps. Jess'll be here if'n you need anything."

Back in the kitchen, Charlie grabbed his jacket from the peg, quietly opened the front door, and slipped out into the morning. He pulled his jacket closer around him in the freezing cold air. He wouldn't be gone long, just a jaunt up the hill, retrieve the gun, and be back here in no time. Jess would never even know that he left.

Stepping softly, Charlie poked his head around the corner in search of the big man. As luck would have it, Jess must've been in the barn or the lean-to, because he wasn't in sight. So Charlie made a beeline through the trees and up the nearest hill. He glanced over his shoulder every now and then, and ran from tree to tree, making sure he stayed covered by their shadows.

Charlie chuckled and said to himself, "Gramps's not the only one with Indian blood in 'im. I'll find Big Blue and be home in—what was that strange saying—'two shakes of a lamb's tail'."

Climbing higher, Charlie stopped once or twice to get his bearings, recognizing landmarks as he climbed. Then before he realized it, he was there, staring at the very place where it had happened. The rock, the brush, and up higher, the timbered fortress that had saved his life. The trees were bare now, their golden leaves scattered across the hillside, but that was where he'd hidden from her, from death.

At the moment, the area didn't remind him of cherished boyhood memories. Those had been replaced by the memory of stone cold fear. He stood there paralyzed. The flashback overtook him with sudden, violent force. His stomach revolted and he heaved twice before vomiting up his breakfast. At first, he was shivering because of the cold, but now, he shook in his boots from raw fear. Gathering his wits, he tried to move forward, to find Big Blue, but his feet were frozen to the earth.

"Just find the gun an' get out," he commanded himself. "Move!" Even then, his boots felt like lead as he picked up one foot and then the other, moving closer to the rock where he'd last held the gun. Sweat poured down his back. He tried to grip the granite boulder with one hand, needing the sense of security, while he scanned the ground with wild eyes.

"I gotta get out of here," he mumbled frantically. Growing frustrated, he rubbed his head with shaking hands. "It ain't here. It ain't here," he groaned.

He glanced back and forth over the hillside, struggling to remember. "I had it in my hand till she screamed at me," he whimpered. "I dropped it when I started up the hill."

He shuffled to the other side of the rock, then froze, blinded with fear. Out of the corner of his eye he saw the brush move. It was happening again! This time, though, there was no escape. He turned his head and tried to focus, but his vision blurred and failed him. He could only make out flickers of a golden shape coming closer. He recognized the heavy footsteps, the familiar sound of breathing as the shape bounded towards him, and the roar of the death warning.

Shaking uncontrollably, he tried to scream, but he only gasped for air as his eyes rolled back into his head and he collapsed on the ground. Feeling nothing, he retreated into the comfort of unconsciousness.

19

CHARLIE AWOKE COVERED WITH DIRT, or so he thought. Arms thrashing, he threw the blankets off and sat up, trying to remember where he was. Then he saw Jess looking down at him.

"Well, 'bout time you woke up, son," Jess said, smiling.

Charlie looked around. "What am I doin' here?"

"How 'bout you tellin' me?" asked Jess. He turned back to the cupboards. "You were goin' to stay with your grandpa in case he opened his eyes, remember?"

Charlie grabbed hold of that thought. "Did Gramps open 'is eyes?" he asked eagerly.

Jess continued his supper fixings. "No," he said. "No, he hasn't yet. He's the same as he was."

Charlie sank back into his blankets and rubbed his head, still trying to clear the mental fog. "Guess I better get up an' get Gramps' supper for 'im, then."

Jess didn't turn from his work. "No need to, Charlie. I took care of your grandpa about an hour ago."

What in the world had happened? Charlie was embarrassed and befuddled. He sat up and pushed the covers off his legs. "Th-thanks, Jess," he stuttered sheepishly.

"How 'bout washin' your hands and gettin' ready for some supper yourself?" said Jess. "It'll be on the table in … two shakes of a lamb's tail."

The phrase stunned Charlie. How funny to hear it again so soon. He got up and slid his blankets back into the corner. Turning towards the basin, he suddenly froze in his tracks. His eyes were focused on the face of the fireplace, just above the mantle. "Where'd you find it?" he whispered.

Jess finally turned and leaned back against the counter, folding his arms across his chest. With wide eyes, Charlie searched Jess's face for an answer.

"I found it at your feet," replied the big man. "And I found you on a hillside, scared pretty near to death."

The boy was dumbfounded. After a moment he collected himself enough to ask, "How'd you get to me before *she* did?"

"There wasn't a *she*, Charlie. It was me comin' out of them bushes." Jess's tone was stern but with an underlying gentleness. "I knew what you were plannin' on doin' the minute you asked to be excused from helpin' with the day's work. In fact, I was there on the hill before you, Charlie … ready to protect you, or help if you'd asked me to, but you got yourself worked up to such a fright, you couldn't see me or hear me talkin' to you."

"You," Charlie whispered. "It was you?"

111

"Yep, it was only me," answered Jess. "That she-bear is sleepin' in a cave somewhere right now." He shoved his hands into his pockets, his eyes reflecting some inward pain. "All you had to do was trust me, son."

Charlie slumped down into the rocking chair and put his hands over his face. "I didn't think you'd help me, Jess. I didn't tell you the truth a few weeks back when I first told you 'bout the bear attack and me losin' Big Blue. I was afraid if I told you the truth, you'd leave. 'Sides that, I didn't want anyone to know what I'd done."

Jess folded his hands in front of him as if in readiness. "Do you want to tell me now?"

Charlie raised his eyes to meet those of the big man. "I reckon," he mumbled. "It's just that I ain't never been alone before, so I was tryin' to do ev'rythin' by myself, tryin' to be the man of the house. I know I prob'ly shoulda run to the Tuttles' farm to get help, but I thought I could handle things. And I didn't want Gramps to wake up and me not be here."

"I understand that, son, and you did a right good job 'round here, but why'd you decide to take your grandpa's gun out?"

Again Charlie looked at him, bewildered. How did he know so much?

Jess continued. "I know you wanted me to think that he gave you permission, but that's not true, is it?"

Charlie closed his eyes and hung his head. "No, sir, it ain't," he confessed. "I gave *myself* permission to carry the gun out. Gramps never did, it was all me."

"Why, Charlie?"

"'Cause, 'cause …" the boy lifted his head again, his wide eyes defensive and pleading. He choked back the tears. "'Cause I was scared, Jess. Can't you see that?" His voice rose a pitch higher. "I was here all alone. It was up to me to take care of ev'rything."

Jess remained calm. Charlie still hadn't come to terms with the matter. "So why didn't you use a gun more familiar to you—your own rifle?"

Charlie kicked a piece of bark across the floor. "'Cause," he stammered. "'Cause I had to prove to Gramps that I could handle 'is gun. *He* thought I was too young, but *I* didn't think so. I knew I couldn't ha' fought off bad guys or Indians with *my* gun. I couldn't ha' defended me and Gramps if I'd 'a had to." Charlie sat back in the rocker and stared out the room's one little window. "I know Gramps told me never to use 'is gun, but he'd been teachin' me to shoot with it, and I thought it'd be all right."

Jess's voice became soft and low. "Was it right?"

Charlie's voice cracked. "No," he whispered. "No, it wasn't. I didn't realize till she charged at me, but I didn't even have the gun loaded. I left here without preparin' the powder or anything." His voice was almost inaudible. "I knew when I was holed up in them trees with that grizzly tryin' to kill me that Gramps'd been right all along. I ain't ready to handle Big Blue. I ain't a man yet."

Jess nodded, and his eyes looked wise and thoughtful. He spoke softly. "That's right, Charlie, you're not a grown man yet. You're a boy, and that's okay. That's the way it's

113

s'posed to be. It takes lots of time and heaps of learnin' for a boy to grow into a man."

Charlie watched the expression on the big man's face. It was a look of understanding, love, and acceptance. Charlie had seen that look in the eyes of Mr. Tuttle one time when Wilbur had done something stupid. He'd broken his father's tool and he'd confessed it to his dad and told him he was sorry. Mr. Tuttle scolded him, but then, with gentle voice and eyes he told him that he hoped he'd learned a lesson and wouldn't do it again.

A wave of relief flooded over Charlie. He was just a boy. He might make stupid choices and mistakes. But he could still find acceptance in the eyes of a man like Jess.

But Jess's face also showed concern, and even sorrow. "Charlie, if your grandpa woke up and walked in here and saw that his gun was missin', what do you think would hurt him the most, that Big Blue was gone or that you'd disobeyed him?"

Charlie sat in silence for a moment, mulling the question around in his head. "I'm sorta like Adam, ain't I, Jess? I disobeyed Gramps like Adam disobeyed God, and I really made a mess of things."

"Like I said, Charlie, sin will do that."

Charlie's despondent gaze fell to the floor. "I'm sorry, Jess," he murmured. "I'm sorry for disobeying Gramps, I'm sorry for losin' Big Blue, and I'm sorry for lyin' to you, not once, but twice. You been nothin' but good to me, and I've not honored that." Charlie looked up. "Can you forgive me, Jess?"

To the boy's surprise, tears welled in the corners of the big man's gray eyes as he whispered, "You're forgiven, Charlie."

Charlie walked over to the soft-hearted mountain man and threw his arms around his wide, chamois-shirted waist. Jess went down on his knees and embraced the boy as tears quietly rolled down his round cheeks and disappeared into his grizzled beard. Charlie could feel the gentle shudder of the big man's strong shoulders.

During supper, Jess filled Charlie in on the details of his trip to Pueblo and Charlie told Jess about his time with Gramps. When supper was over and everything was back in its proper place, they pulled out their bedrolls and relaxed in front of the fire. Jess stretched his arms and yawned a mountain-man sized yawn. "I feel better knowin' that the cupboards are full." He rubbed his tired eyes. "The snow could start to fall any day now."

Charlie lay in his usual position, flat on his back with his hands behind his head. "Thanks for findin' Big Blue, Jess," he said. "Thanks for protectin' me and bringin' me home, for cuttin' all the wood, and for, well, for ev'rything. I don't know what I'd 'a done without you."

Jess smiled. "Well, Charlie, I thank you for givin' me a place to stay warm an' all. If it weren't for folks like you and your grandpa, I'd be up in the hills somewhere, shiverin' like a new born pup, I reckon. But most of all, I thank you for trustin' me."

"I'm glad you're here so I can trust you." Charlie was

silent a moment, then continued. "Jess, I been readin' to Gramps. Sometimes I read from the Scrooge story and other times from the Bible. The other night I read 'bout Jesus in the manger. Did you know there's gonna be three of us havin' a birthday here in just a couple of days?"

"Three of us?"

"Yep," replied Charlie. "Jesus, you, and me. It's almost Christmas, Jess, and it's gonna be nice with you here."

Charlie stared at the ceiling. The reflection of the fire danced in his eyes. Jess smiled at the boy as if he was thinking of a secret.

Outside, snowflakes quietly drifted to the earth, covering the ground with a blanket of pure, crystalline softness.

The next morning, Jess filled Goliath's bucket with fresh oats. "Well, I'll be," he said to the horse. "I guess we got back just in time, ol' boy. We got us a passel of snow last night. Did you stay warm enough in this here little box?" Fixing his big brown eyes on Jess, Goliath nickered his affection and assurance that he was fine.

Charlie was at his grandpa's side. He climbed up onto the feather mattress and made himself comfortable beside Gramps and started to read the Christmas book where he'd left off last time. Again, the old man's eyes fluttered as Charlie read. Today his color radiated hews of pink and his breathing sounded almost normal. It would be so natural for Gramps to just open his eyes and look around. Charlie knew he was in there somewhere, fighting to get out.

Charlie stopped reading and slid off the bed. He leaned in close to his grandpa's ear. "I reckon I'll hafta tell you this again when you wake up, Gramps, but right now, I gotta get things off my chest. I know you told me that I was too young to handle your gun, but I got scared and didn't listen. I took Big Blue out not too long ago and, well, I lost it. But ... but don't go gettin' excited or nothin', 'cause I went lookin' for it the other day and, well, Jess helped me find it, so it's back up on the mantle now where it belongs. I just wanted you to know that I'm sorry for not listenin' to you. I don't ever want you to think you can't trust me again."

Gramps' eyelids flickered.

"I hope you can hear me, Gramps," he whispered. "With all my heart I'm sorry and I won't disobey you ever again."

The realization of his sin tugged at his heart. He'd been wrong to disobey Gramps, he knew that, but what Jess had told him about needing Jesus as his Savior suddenly made sense. He was no different than Adam. His disobedience was sin, too, and what did Jess say, sin separates us from God. "I don't want to be separated from God," he whispered.

Laying his head on his grandpa's chest, Charlie closed his eyes. "Dear Jesus," he whispered, "I really don't know where to start, so I guess I'll just right out ask for your forgiveness. I know if Gramps knew 'bout my sin it'd hurt 'im to the core, but I guess it hurts you even more. You even had to die 'cause of it." Tears rolled down Charlie's cheeks. "I don't want nothin' to separate me from you. I know now what it's like to be all alone, and I don't ever wanna feel that way again. I wanna know that even if I can't see you, you're always with me and won't ever leave me. Jesus, please forgive me for my sins and come into my heart." Charlie lifted his head and wiped the tears off his face. "Amen," he whispered.

At that moment, outside in the lean-to Jess listened, a broad smile crinkling his face. As one hand slid down Goliath's silken mane, followed by the stroke of a brush, the mountain man seemed to be listening to some far-away sound, maybe angels singing somewhere in the distance.

20

ON THE DAY OF CHRISTMAS EVE, SNOW covered the landscape and glistened in the sun. Jess, who had been hunting since before sunrise, returned to the cabin with a deer and two rabbits strapped to his saddle, and with a big evergreen tied behind.

Charlie had been standing on the back doorstep, watching the mountain man and his horse come down from the hills. As they approached, he waved and yelled, "What's that for, Jess?"

"Whoa, boy," said Jess, as he reined his horse to a stop. "Well, good mornin', Charlie." He turned in the huge leather saddle and pointed toward the tree Goliath had been dragging behind him. "This here is a real, bona fide Christmas tree!"

Charlie's eyes grew large. "A Christmas tree! I haven't had a Christmas tree since—" He stopped to think, then proclaimed, "—not since Grandma was alive."

The memories sparked his excitement. "She'd ask me

to collect pinecones an' holly, then we'd tuck 'em in the branches, and then she'd pop us some corn and we'd make long strings of popcorn an' wind 'em 'round n' 'round the tree," he chattered, almost nonstop. "An' Grandma had some special plates that she'd bring out just for Christmas dinner—an' Easter, too. ... I wonder where them dishes went to?"

Jess chuckled. Deftly he untied the rope from the saddle horn and pulled the tree to the cabin door. Charlie watched as Jess hung the deer carcass from a tree branch. Then he secured Goliath in his lean-to. Finally, he grabbed the evergreen and hauled it inside with just a couple of bounding steps. The tree filled the doorway, much as Jess himself did. When Jess set the tree upright in a corner of the cabin, it stood even taller than the mountain man himself. Its tip almost touched the ceiling. Instantly the little cabin was filled with the pungent fragrance of pine.

"It's beautiful," Charlie whispered.

Slapping pieces of bark from his hands, Jess went to the basin to wash off the sap. "Well, Charlie, this is just the start. When I went to town the other day, I was anticipatin' this moment, so I bought some bobbles for our tree. After breakfast, how 'bout we dig those out and see if we can really make 'er shine?"

21

CHARLIE JUMPED UP AND DOWN FOR JOY as Jess pulled the cloth sack from the cupboard and dumped its contents onto the kitchen table. The treasure consisted of twenty little white candles, twenty little tin drip pans, and—to Charlie's particular delight—eleven red-and-white striped peppermint sticks. Something was missing, though. Jess picked up the sack and reached his large hand inside to pull out the crowning jewel, a tin star to put on the very top. Charlie loved it. He loved it all.

Laying the sack aside, Jess pointed to a peppermint stick. "I have to confess, Charlie," he said. "I really bought twelve of them candy sticks, but I ate one on the trip back." His eyes twinkled. "An' it was mighty good-tastin'!"

Charlie laughed. "That's okay, Jess. It's your birthday, too."

"Why, yes it is," he said with a clap of his hands. "Now, let's get started on makin' this place look festive."

Jess pulled a thin piece of smoldering wood out of the

fireplace and lit one of the candles. He tipped the candle and let the melting wax drip onto one of the little pans. Then he set the candle in the soft wax and blew out the little flame.

"That's how it's done," he said. Charlie took another piece of glowing cinder wood from the grate and followed Jess's lead. Before long, the twenty candles stood at attention all over the giant evergreen, cheerfully adorning its branches.

Charlie carefully placed the peppermint sticks on various branches. Jess took the empty calico sack and started to tear long, thin strips.

"What're you doin' that for?" asked Charlie.

"I'm makin' some bows for our tree."

"Bows? You mean like Mary Lou wears on 'er pigtails?"

"Yep."

Charlie thought for a minute. "I know where we can find some shiny ribbons for makin' bows."

Jess stopped ripping the sack and said, "You do?"

Charlie nodded. "Yep. Want me to go get 'em?"

"Well, are they somethin' your grandpa won't mind us usin'?"

"I don't think he'll mind," answered Charlie. "They just been sittin' in the drawer."

"Well, then, go get 'em and let me see."

In the bedroom Charlie pulled open the top drawer of the chest. Folded in a corner were seven silk ribbons, each about twelve inches long. He hesitated a moment, then picked them up and cradled them in his hands as gently as if they were baby birds. Then he took the ribbons to Jess and laid them with a flourish on the table. "Here they are."

"These are beautiful, Charlie. Did they belong to your grandma?"

Charlie nodded slightly, suddenly unable to speak.

Jess tied a blue ribbon into a perky bow with his large fingers, then he got up and tied the bow to the tree. "This bow's gentle and soft just like your grandma was, huh, Charlie?"

Charlie touched the silken material. "Yeah. She was gentle ... always singin' hymns real soft while she worked. Even the birds liked 'er singin'. They didn't even fly away when she'd hang out the laundry. They just perched on the clothesline poles an' watched 'er an' kept on chirpin'."

"Did she wear these ribbons in her hair?"

"Not since I remember. I just remember she had long, white hair pulled back in a bun. But ev'ry night before bed she'd let it down and brush it out. She always brushed her hair a hundert times." Charlie cast a shy smile at Jess. "That's how I learnt to count, by countin' to a hundert along with Grandma ev'ry night."

"She sure was good to you, Charlie."

"Yeah. She was good to ev'ryone. An' she was always so glad to find new baby things growin', like fluffy chicks or newborn calves or spring flowers comin' up volunteer. Didn't matter where they came up, she wanted to leave 'em there and help 'em grow."

"She'd be mighty happy to see how you've been growin',

Charlie." The giant man regarded the boy with soft eyes for a moment, then he said, "Here, son, why don't you go ahead an' put the rest of the ribbons on the tree—make some red an' pink an' purple bows for our tree. I need to stoke the fire, and then check on Goliath."

Charlie nodded and picked up a red ribbon. Jess stepped outside and Charlie sat in the rocker. Starting on the knot, he was soon absorbed in memories. Jess let him have as much time as he figured the boy needed.

When Jess returned he asked, "Charlie, would you like to put the star on top of the tree?"

"Sure, but I can't reach way up there, even if I stood on a chair."

"Sure you can. I'll just hold you up there."

Charlie took the star and Jess hoisted the boy up with one strong arm so he could reach clear to the ceiling and place the star right on top of the tip-top of the tree. Then Jess set him back down and the two admired their beautiful Christmas tree.

"The star really makes the difference, doesn't it, Jess?" Charlie noted. "Now it's beautiful from top to bottom."

"Sometimes stars make a big difference, Charlie. Often they lend a hand at guidin' or offerin' direction, and they form designs in the sky that people use to measure time an' distance. Then, they add that finishin' touch to a Christmas tree."

Charlie smiled and enjoyed the peaceful moment.

"Speakin' of stars, Charlie. I wonder if you'd step out on

the front step with me for a minute? I'd like to show you somethin'."

"Okay, Jess. What is it?"

They grabbed their jackets and stepped out the door. Jess pointed to a bright star high in the sky to their left. "That there is the north star, Charlie. This time of the year folks like to call it the Christmas star, 'cause it seems to shine a little brighter now."

"Well, I'll be," whispered the boy. "Is it the same star that shined above the manger when Jesus was born?"

"Perhaps," said Jess. "But even if it isn't, the two stars have a lot in common."

"Like what?" asked the boy.

"The Good Book says that the Christmas star led men to Jesus after He was born. It also says that God's throne sits northward in the heavens. So in a sense the stars still provide a map to God."

Charlie gazed at the star. "Wow," he whispered. "You mean to say that God is sittin' right 'bout there?" He pointed to the northern sky.

"Yep," said Jess.

"Well, now that I know where He's sittin', I'll know where to look when I'm talkin' to 'im."

Jess let out a hearty laugh, but Charlie didn't take his eyes off the star. "God's throne," he whispered.

"God's not really as far away as that star is, son. We can use that as a guide just like the shepherds an' wisemen did a long time ago. But in reality, He's standin' right here next to you. In fact, He's really just as close as your own heart."

Charlie placed his hand in Jess's and smiled up at him.

Jess continued. "Jesus promised to always be with you, and He'll never forsake you." He looked down at the boy with piercing but warm gray eyes. "You'll never need to be all alone again, Charlie."

Charlie wanted to believe that. "Never?" he asked.

Jess leaned down and scooped the boy up into his powerful arms. He looked steadily into Charlie's eyes. Then he smiled and his face crinkled with smile lines. His eyes twinkled as if he was thinking of a delightful secret. "Never, young man. I promise you that."

22

CHRISTMAS DAWNED GRAY AND COLD. Wind blew across the prairie and whistled round the corners of the cabin. The gusts picked up tumbleweeds and tossed them rolling over the snow-covered ground. Charlie didn't care. The sounds of the howling wind didn't bother him anymore.

Jess made oatmeal, adding some of the plump sweet raisins he'd picked up in Pueblo. He called it their birthday breakfast. Charlie ate until he was full and satisfied. Then he put some mushy oatmeal in a cup, removed the raisins, and watered it down to a soup so Gramps could swallow it. While Gramps' oatmeal cooled he asked, "What're we gonna do today, Jess?"

Jess was busy pulling out new bags of flour, spices, and sugar from the cupboards and sitting them on the table with the milk, butter, and eggs that he'd brought in from the root cellar earlier.

"Well, son, after chores, I think we oughta do some

cookin'. It's our birthdays and it's Christmas, so I think we oughta bake bread rolls, make us some fancy sugar cookies an' apple pie, and roast a big venison sirloin with taters an' carrots. How's that sound to you?"

"Sounds great to me!" exclaimed Charlie.

After the boy fed Gramps, he and Jess got down to business. Charlie helped peel vegetables, mix dough, and sprinkle sugar across the face of the golden cookies.

The pie, cookies, vegetables and meat were each cooked or baked in the various wrought-iron kettles, skillets, and pots that hung on hooks in the fireplace.

The house filled with mouth-watering aromas. Granted, the eleven-year-old boy made more of a mess and ate more cookie dough than he should have, but Jess offered no reprimands. After all, it was Christmas and their birthdays!

Lunchtime was short, just long enough to feed Gramps and wash down their quick sandwiches with milk, and then the two were back at work, mixing, blending, and whipping up their evening feast.

So the day passed happily, full of anticipation, and it turned into a cold but clear Christmas night.

"Charlie," said Jess. "Why don't you get your grandpa's Bible and read the Christmas story from the book of Luke while I finish up the last of the cookin'?"

"Sure, Jess."

Grabbing the Bible from Gramps' nightstand, Charlie read the passage, with Jess's help on some of the words, smiling when he got to the part about the bright star shining in the eastern sky. When he had finished, he closed the book and laid it on the small table beside the rocker.

"That's real good readin', son," said Jess. "Makes me right proud."

Charlie grinned. "I'm glad you been teachin' me. Makes a big difference when you know how to read."

"Sure does," answered Jess. "You'll use that skill for the rest of your life."

Charlie jumped up and gathered the plates from the cupboard and began to set the table, anticipating the meal that was soon to be served.

"Why don't you use what's in the box under the counter?" asked Jess.

Charlie followed Jess's glance and saw a wooden box sticking part way out from beneath the work space.

"But that there's just a box of my clothes," he exclaimed, giggling.

Jess didn't turn from his work. "I think you should take a closer look."

Charlie obediently laid down the forks he was holding and walked over to the box. Wiping away the dust, he saw words stamped across the lid. He sounded out the words, reading out loud: "*Fine China, Saint Louis, Missouri.*" Charlie's mouth fell open. He gave the lid a tug and it slid smoothly off the box. There, nestled in tufts of straw were Grandma's special dishes!

"Jess," he gasped.

The big man turned and smiled. "Surprised?"

Charlie ran to him and gave him a tight hug. "You bet I am."

The mountain man laughed. "That was the intent."

Charlie picked up a plate and wiped off the clinging bits of straw. The gold-trimmed opal china sparkled, revealing the rainbow of colors within its pearly glaze. "Merry Christmas, Grandma," Charlie whispered.

Charlie set the table with the beautiful dishes while Jess cleared away all the spices and cooking utensils. Jess put the bread dough in a covered iron kettle and secured it on one of the large hooks in the fireplace. He gently pushed it back into the heat of the fire, close to the hot stones. Then he lit the candles on the tree and another one that he'd placed on the windowsill. The cabin resonated with the sights and smells that come only with Christmas. Fresh-baked goods mingled with the scent of pine while twenty soft-flickering candles enhanced the firelight like a small band of carolers.

Charlie sat in the rocking chair and slowly pushed with his toes, starting a rhythmic motion back and forth. He looked up at Big Blue, hanging snuggly above the mantel. Then he gazed with satisfaction at his Christmas tree. He felt secure and at peace. Jess cleaned up the counters and finished setting the hot dishes of food on the table, just waiting for the bread.

"I wonder what Wilbur's doin' right now," said Charlie as he studied the flickering lights on the tree. "I bet it's noisy at the Tuttles' house." He paused and inhaled deeply. "But it sure can't smell any nicer."

"Got a passel of kids, do they?" asked Jess.

"Four," said Charlie. "Four kids with their ma an' pa, all livin' in a one-room cabin."

"That'd be a full house," said Jess, chuckling. Then he turned from the counter. "Oh, yeah. Speakin' of Ma an' Pa Tuttle, I ran into them when I was in Pueblo. They were just comin' out of the general store when I was headin' in and they asked if I'd do 'em a favor and deliver a package."

Charlie stopped the rocker with the heel of his boot. "A package? For who?"

"Well, it's under the tree, so why don't you see for yourself?"

Charlie looked and sure enough, a bundle of brown paper was peeking out from beneath the lowest branch of the pine. He scrambled from the rocker, landed on his knees in front of the tree, and pulled out the package. There was a little card tied to it with string. It read:

> *To Charlie,*
> *Happy birthday and merry Christmas.*
> *The Tuttle Family*

"For me?" squealed Charlie, his sparkling eyes as big as saucers. "Can I open it, Jess?"

"Yep, I reckon you can." The big man smiled.

Charlie tore the paper away and held up a brand new, green-and-gold plaid woolen shirt. "Oh my goodness," he whispered. "I ain't never had nothin' this fancy."

Jess gave a low whistle. "That's a mighty fine shirt there, Charlie."

Charlie was staring at the gift and Jess cleared his throat. "Well, go ahead an' try it on, son."

Charlie unbuttoned and pulled off his worn denim shirt and tossed it to the floor. He thrust his arms into the sleeves of the new garment and buttoned it as fast as his fingers could fly. He held his arms out and measured the sleeves, then smoothed the front.

"Looks mighty fine to me," Jess said. "Those Tuttles are kind folks. And they must think highly of you, son."

Charlie absentmindedly picked at a piece of fuzz on the shirt sleeve. "Yeah," he answered, "one time Mrs. Tuttle said she loved me just like I was one of her very own."

Charlie sat back down in the rocker, lost in thought. A smile slowly inched across his freckled face as he pushed back on the rocker, relaxed, and felt his eyes grow heavy.

"Jess?" he asked sleepily.

"Yep, Charlie."

"Thanks for makin' this the best Christmas ever."

Moving to the front door, Jess reached for his buckskin jacket and his coonskin cap. He put his hand on the latch, then paused to turn back toward the boy. "You made it special for me too, Charlie," he said. "In fact, you gave me the best Christmas gift—and birthday gift!—that I could ask for."

Before Charlie could ask what that was, Jess continued, "I'm gonna step outside now."

Charlie yawned. "Okay, Jess." He figured Jess was going to check on Goliath or maybe use the outhouse.

23

AFTER JESS CLOSED THE DOOR BEHIND him, Charlie got up and went to check on Gramps, one last time before dinner. But at the bedroom door he came to a dead stop, staring in disbelief. There on the bed lay Gramps, but he was fully awake and supporting himself on one elbow, squinting his eyes, trying to bring things into focus. Charlie couldn't believe it. "Gramps!" he yelled. "You're awake!"

The old man looked up and his big smile was once again hanging from those high cheekbones. "I am, son," he said, and it was so good to hear his voice. "I'm wide awake, Charlie," he added.

The boy ran as fast as he could and jumped onto the bed, landing in his grandpa's arms, crying with joy, hugging him tightly, all the while whispering, "Thank you, God, thank you, thank you."

Covering the boy's face with kisses, Gramps thanked God, too. He held Charlie in his feeble arms while his grandson told him all about Jess and Goliath. He told him of learning to read and cook and of helping with the chores to get ready for winter. He told Gramps everything, barely stopping to take a breath.

"Charlie," said Gramps, "is this Jess a great big fella with salt 'n pepper hair an' beard?"

The boy looked surprised. "That's right, Gramps. How did you know? You don't know 'im, do you?"

"The old man's eyes glazed a little as he seemed to wander back in time for a moment. "I do," he finally replied. "I met Jess back when your pa had 'is accident. He befriended your grandma an' me and helped us through that terrible time."

The boy was incredulous. "You sure it's the same Jess?"

"Don't think there's another quite like 'im, son." He looked directly into his grandson's eyes. Then he lifted a weak hand and ruffled his hair until it poked out in all directions. Charlie laughed and hugged his grandpa again.

Sitting back on his heels, Charlie thought of a question he'd been wanting to ask. Gramps might be the only one who knew the answer. Charlie swallowed, then asked, "Gramps, did my ma an' pa love me?"

Grandpa stroked Charlie's cheek with a long, thin finger, following the outline of his thin face till he stopped at the boy's chin. "More'n anything in this world," he whispered. "Your ma didn't get to be with you too long, but even before you was born, she called you her 'little bundle from Heaven.' And your pa, well, up till the day he died, you was his pride and joy."

Charlie lowered his eyes.

"And me," continued the old man, "well, the day your Grandma an' I went back to Saint Louie to bury your pa beside your ma, then bring you back here to live with us, you became our pride and joy."

Charlie leaned in and rested his head against his grandpa's chest.

"I missed you so much, Gramps. I didn't think you were gonna make it, and it woulda been my fault, too."

Gramps held his boy tightly. "Not so, Charlie, not so. My life was always in God's hands. The decision was His to make an' His alone."

Gramps let go and held Charlie's shoulders, fixing his gaze into the boy's eyes, "I heard what you did with Big Blue, Charlie," he started. "And I heard you say you was sorry."

Charlie bowed his head and whispered, "I really am sorry, Gramps."

The old man pulled Charlie's chin upward until their eyes met again. "I heard your prayer for forgiveness. We've all done wrong, son. I've prayed that same prayer myself. And rest assured, boy, there ain't nothin' more important to me on this earth than you. I love you more'n that gun, this cabin, or anything else. You know that?"

Charlie looked into the tired, gentle brown eyes and nodded.

"But the Father loves you even more'n I do. You might not understand it all right now, but some day you will. All that happened was just a part of His plan."

"His plan?" Charlie's eyes grew round.

"It's hard for you to understand all this right now, just like it was for me back when your pa died, and at times even now I have questions. But all the things that happen in our lives, God uses for His plan. I know God will make sense of it all someday, but till then we'll just keep trustin' Him."

"That's the same thing Jess told me, Gramps."

"And I suggest you take his lessons to heart, son. He's well-acquainted with truth."

Charlie grew quiet, thinking of the things Jess had tried to teach him over the past several weeks.

Then Gramps—stiff and weak, grimacing a little because of aching joints—began to inch his feet towards the edge of the bed. "Now I'd like to get up and stretch, even for just a minute." He groaned as his depleted muscles searched for the strength demanded of them. "Maybe I can visit with Jess a while. I'd sure like to see 'im again."

Charlie sprang to his feet. "Sure, Gramps, I'll help you."

The old man put a trembling hand on his grandson's shoulder and leaned on him as little by little he rose from the bed to his feet and shuffled into the other room, where he eased into the rocking chair. Then he sighed.

Once Gramps was comfortable, Charlie turned towards the door. "Jess is just outside checkin' on 'is horse, I think. I'll go fetch 'im."

Gramps let out a low whistle. "What a beautiful tree, Charlie. You and Jess really did 'er up right. Smells good, too."

Charlie smiled. "I still can hardly believe it," he said.

But Gramps didn't seem to hear as he sat there staring at the tree. Pointing with a feeble hand, he whispered, "Are those your grandma's ribbons?"

"Yessir. I didn't think you'd mind."

Grandpa stared at the silk bows hanging delicately from the tree. Tears filled his eyes. "Don't mind at all, son."

Charlie smiled. On his way to the door, something on the table caught his eye. It was a package wrapped in brown paper. The words, "To Charlie" were handwritten across the front. Curious, he picked it up and began tearing off the brown paper.

As the wrapping fell away, a beautiful new Bible slowly emerged in Charlie's hands, and right on the front cover, stamped in gold, was his name, Charles Edward Smith. It was the prettiest book he'd ever seen. The scent of the leather cover filled his nostrils as he carefully turned the delicate pages, looking at the verses in their fine print. Turning to the inside cover, he noticed a handwritten inscription. Moving closer to the lamp, he read:

> *To my friend Charlie,*
> *This is God's BIG plan. Read it, learn it, and*
> *trust it always. It will never steer you wrong.*
> *With love,*
> *Jethro Ezekiel Samson Uriah Samuels*

Staring at the letters, Charlie whispered, "Gramps! Look. Jess's initials spell J-E-S-U-S." Grandpa didn't reply. Resting his head against the back of the rocker, he closed his eyes and smiled.

Laying the Bible on the table, Charlie bolted to the door and ran out into the snow. "Jess!" he yelled. "Jess, where are you?"

The night was black but the snow-blanketed earth gleamed brightly in the starlight. The wind whipped up from the prairie, but Charlie didn't notice. To his call there was no reply, just the sound of his own voice echoing through the trees that huddled together on the hillside as if trying to keep the cold from entering their domain.

"Jess!" he yelled again. He turned and ran to the lean-to. "Jess, where are you?" Clutching the doorframe, he peered into the shed. It was empty.

Tears stung his eyes. He spun on his heels and ran towards the barn. Then he stopped abruptly. Jess couldn't be back there; there were no footprints. He ran back to the lean-to and looked around again. The only footprints in the snow were those that Charlie himself had left when he came out from the cabin.

Charlie scanned the darkness. "He's gone," he said out loud. "Jess an' Goliath are gone."

Standing in the dark, he looked around at the emptiness and waited for loneliness to flood him as it had done so many times before. He waited to hear the haunting echoes from the trees laughing at his weakness, or the wind howling at his ignorance, but none of it ever came. This time was different. Looking up at the brightest star, he remembered: Jess wasn't really gone. He promised he would never leave him and he'd taught Charlie to look for a reminder in the sky—like a promise—reminding him that he could talk to

138

Jesus any time…. Because now Jesus lived in his heart.

Gramps stood framed in the cabin doorway. "Come back into the house, Charlie."

Reflecting on his discovery, Charlie trudged through the snow back to his grandpa and took his hand. Before turning into the house, Gramps paused and looked skyward. "Look at that sky," he said. "So clear. And look over yonder, Charlie. Why, that's the Christmas star."

"Yep," agreed Charlie. He gazed at the star again and felt a surge of excitement. "I never did ask 'im to finish tellin' me the long version of his name, Gramps. I just got use to callin' 'im Jess."

Gramps was still looking at the stars. "You were missin' the '-*us*' in his name, huh?" he whispered.

Charlie looked up at the old man, but his grandpa's gaze stayed fixed on the sky. He was remembering something from the past. "That's what he told me years back, when he gave me *my* Bible." He was talking more to himself now than to the boy. "Said it was all because of his love for us." He grinned down at Charlie. That's *us* spelled '*u-s*'."

Charlie turned his face back toward the heavens. "Oh," he whispered. "That's what he meant when he said I gave 'im the best Christmas present anyone could ask for."

Gramps smiled and nodded. "Yep, son, I reckon that's what he meant."

At that moment, a gust of wind rushed across the prairie, hitting the trees, whipping the upper branches into motion; whistling down to Charlie and Gramps. From somewhere on the wind, Jess's voice seemed to whisper in the boy's ear, "Happy birthday, Charlie."

The boy smiled and squeezed his grandpa's hand. Looking up at the star, Charlie whispered, "Happy birthday, Jesus."

Acknowledgments

I sincerely thank: Catherine Lawton of Cladach Publishing for seeing the diamond in the rough and for her willingness to "trust in the Lord" while taking a chance with this first-time author; my husband, Blaine Gallup, who gave me direction in the research, advice on the plot, and encouragement when I was discouraged; Char Wixson, a dear friend, who edited through laughter and tears, letting me know I was on the right track; Amy Feriozzi, who freely offered her advice and assistance; and my family and friends who believed.